To Erica,

Blessings

Brianne Hugo

1

Days of Our Future

{Sequel to The Unforgotten Past}

Enjoy ♡

Love, Pop Pop & Nana

By Brianne E. Pryor

*In loving honor of my grandparents,
Gerald and Faye Pryor, for their love and
support and for always pointing
me to Christ.*

The Sequel

"For I know the plans I have for you," says the Lord. "Plans to prosper you and not to harm you. Plans to give you hope and a future."
Jeremiah 29:11

1923

She was only twelve, a girl in her prime years of childhood. She was full of life and adventure and her heart wanted nothing more than to be free; free of what she was, of what her family was. She was determined to take that freedom for herself rather than wait for fate to change her life of abuse and hatred. She looked down at her sleeping twin brother who lay beside her on their cot. His red hair matted to his forehead with sweat drawn by the sticky summer heat. Looking at him she realized how much she cared for him, loved him even, and she wondered if he loved her, if he would miss her when she was gone.

They were all her flesh and blood but this boy, he was her twin brother, he was her only friend, the one she protected with every once of her power against the rest of the world which always seemed to be against them. How could she leave this boy alone to face their family of killers and thieves? How could she leave her own brother whom she had looked after her entire life? The only person left in the world that she loved and that loved her.

I wish I could bring you, her heart yearned as she watched him sleep. But however she desired to awaken him and tell him of her plan to escape, she could not. She could not offer him a life always on the run. She could not take the chance that he would not be strong enough to survive. And above all, she could not risk that he would grow to become the men their father and older brothers were. As much as it pained her, she had no choice but to leave him behind.

There was no way for this child to save her brother from their life, but she had to save herself. They already hated her, she could not wait until they had had enough of her. She had to get out. She could not waist another day of her life here in this lonely place full of killers, thieves and abusers. People she was forced to call her family; her flesh and blood.

Well no more.

Tonight she would rid herself of them forever. She was going to leave and face a world she knew nothing of and she was going to do it alone. She was going to get them out of her life forever...or so she thought.

ONE

Arrival

September 21st, 1929. 1:30pm. Dallas, Texas

The whistle blew, brakes squealed, and white steam shot
into the air as the train pulled into the station and came to
a halt next to the crowded platform. It was a hot summer
afternoon. White clouds loomed overhead in the blue
Texas sky. A throng of people were gathered at the station
awaiting the passengers who now filed off the train in
endless streams. Some were greeted by friends and loved
ones, others by business associates or neighbors. Some
disembarked in big groups with their family members or
friends.
The warmth of the greetings caused young LooAnne Nash
to feel even more alone as she also stepped off the train.
Laying a mindful hand on her roll of red hair as the wind
from the platform blew against her freckled face, LooAnne
sighed in discontentment. At eighteen years old, she had
traveled alone to Dallas from Decatur, Texas, her home
since birth, to attend school.
As the niece and heiress of the well-known Texas

millionaire, Rick Nash, it had become imperative that she gain a further education for her future holdings of the Nash fortune.

Her uncle, an astute businessman and well respected throughout the country, had raised LooAnne since the age of twelve. She was the daughter of his younger sister who had eloped when she was but seventeen with Jason Luther, a wanted thief throughout the area. The young couple had taken refuge in the unkempt home of Jason's ruthless family, all of whom were wanted by the Decatur police for numerous crimes ranging from pocket picking to multiple murders. But whenever anyone in the small town had tried to take the Luther's in hand most of the lawmen were either killed or seriously wounded. LooAnne had been born into this family of terrors as Beth Luther and had been trained by them to rob and kill as a primary way of life. But after the untimely death of her parents she had run away from her family's wrath and cruelty and unknowingly crossed from Luther land onto the land of the great Rick Nash who had just happened to be walking alone in his back fields. Separated by miles of farmland and certain that she had gotten lost in the thick woods, LooAnne had no idea that this man she had happened upon was her uncle. Fearing what he might do, she had not given him enough time to lay hands on her before she ran. Her uncle had long before suffered the loss of his wife and two children and now, being a very lonely and grief stricken man, had taken off after the young Luther, not knowing who she was but feeling compelled to chase her. She, however, outran him and leaped a creek which he attempted after her but had lost his footing and strained his wrist.

At first LooAnne had taken this chance to run but she had not gone far before guilt gripped her and she knew that she had to make sure this man was alright.

It was not long after their first meeting that Ricky realized who she was and revealed his own name to his new found niece. Knowing instantly that he was her mother's brother LooAnne found herself in a situation she had never imagined and her uncle finding someone to brighten his loneliness. Because of the terrible Luther reputation LooAnne changed her name from Beth Luther to LooAnne Nash and was hidden at the Nash Estate until her uncle thought it safe to make her existence known without the Luthers realizing who she really was. Now thought by the public to be the daughter of her uncle's younger brother, Robert, she was safely hidden right under the nose of her father's family.

No one knew why she was living with Ricky Nash and not her supposed father and mother but they had too much respect for the Nash's to question it, so it went unquestioned for what LooAnne and her uncle hoped was forever. Their worst thought being was that the now scattered Luther's would come after their runaway, take her back and punish her harshly for leaving, taking their abilities and secrets with her.

This was one of the thoughts that weighed heavily on LooAnne's mind as she stood alone at the station, watching the busy crowd mill about. She had never left Decatur before for fear of running into the Luther's but now that she was out of school Ricky had convinced her to go further in her education, to learn more about the business industry and be better prepared when the time came for her to inherit her uncle's fortune.

"Here's your suitcases, ma-am," said a porter as he sat them down at her feet and tipped his hat. "Can I call you a taxicab, Miss Nash?"

LooAnne looked around and then asked, "How far is the university from here?"

"About a mile down that way, ma-am," he pointed down one of the streets that ran beside the depot.

"You'd better call a cab then if you don't mind?"

"Not one bit."

LooAnne smiled kindly, "Thank you."

The porter tipped his hat again and disappeared into the crowd. LooAnne picked up her suitcase and made her way to a bench where she planned to wait for the cab. She sat her luggage next to her on the ground and removed her gloves which she stuffed in her skirt pocket. LooAnne nervously began fiddling with her freckled fingers, being careful not to lose her uncle's precious golden ring, a small trinket only his closest family members could use to gain access to his home and belongings.

A man in a tall hat took a seat next to her and nodded politely, setting his briefcase on the space between them. She nodded back and immediately realized that she had started chewing her now jagged fingernails. LooAnne huffed at herself and laid her hands firmly in her lap where she was determined to keep them.

"Bill!" came the happy cry of a young woman which drew LooAnne's attention. The man next to her immediately got to his feet and the woman, about LooAnne's age, threw her arms around his neck in animation.

"Take it easy, Cath," the man chuckled, "I've only been gone a week."

"I know, but we missed you!"

12

The man looked to be in his early twenties and shared so many of the young lady's pretty features that LooAnne assumed them to be brother and sister. She took his arm and together they started off, chatting merrily. LooAnne looked down at her hands and sighed, she wished that she had someone here in this strange city to welcome her as that man had. It was then that LooAnne noticed the man's briefcase sitting next to her on the bench. She looked up immediately and could still see the man and his sister walking down the road. LooAnne took hold of the briefcase and of her own luggage and raced after the two. She easily dodged all the pedestrians still at the station and caught the siblings just as they were about to cross the street.

"Excuse me, sir," she called as she ran up on them. The two turned and their questioning stares disappeared when they saw the briefcase. "You forgot this," LooAnne said as she handed it to him.

"Oh thank ya, ma-am," the man said gratefully. "I sure woulda missed that. Good thing you spotted it."

"My pleasure," LooAnne smiled.

The man suddenly frowned, "Ya know," he said, "you look mighty familiar. Have we met before by any chance?"

LooAnne smiled knowingly, "No I'm afraid not, but you do know me, my reputation anyway, I'm LooAnne Nash."

The eyes of the man and his sister widened, "I knew I'd seen you somewhere," he smiled. "It's a pleasure, Miss Nash. I'm Bill Morrison and this is my sister Cathy."

LooAnne shook hands with the two and said that it was a pleasure to meet them as well.

"I never imagined I'd ever meet one of the Nash family," Cathy Morrison said. She was all smiles and had a very pretty face which was framed with short, brown hair that curled at her neck. Her eyes were the exact shade her hair was and they sparkled with a kindness LooAnne immediately took to.

"I'm afraid I'm not as interesting as all that," she said. "I'm glad I could save your bag, Mr. Morrison."

The young man smiled, "So am I."

"We surely didn't expect to have the Nash heiress come running after us with our lost luggage," Cathy declared. "Bill owns one of the banks in town and he needs every little thing he carries in there."

"Well I'm glad I could help."

"I wish we could repay you, Miss Nash," Cathy said cheerily.

"Oh, please don't think of it. I'm glad I could help. I'll miss my cab if I don't hurry back."

"Oh those cabs are much too expensive. I've got an idea," Cathy said enthusiastically. "Bill's gotta get to work and I haven't had lunch yet, can I treat you, Miss Nash? I know all the best diners."

LooAnne smiled, "I really don't expect anything in return for the bag."

"Oh I know, but I hate eating alone and I know Bill's gotta work so would you please do me the honor?"

LooAnne knew that this was the chance she had been waiting for, a chance to have some friends in Dallas. She smiled at Cathy Morrison and said, "Thank you, Miss Morrison, I am kind of hungry after my trip from Decatur."

"It's settled then," Cathy said, cheerily. "We'll see ya later, Bill." She took LooAnne's suitcase in one hand and LooAnne's arm in the other and together they made their way through the crowded streets. Cathy knew them well and she led LooAnne straight to a diner on the corner of two streets which had four circular tables sitting under an awning outside, one of which Cathy decided upon. "This okay?" she asked as she sat LooAnne's suitcase down.

"Just fine," LooAnne said as she took her seat across from Cathy. "This city is so big," she commented looking about her at the tall buildings and flashing lights.

"Oh you'll love it," Cathy assured her. "Are you planning on being here long?"

LooAnne sighed, "For the majority of the next four years I'm afraid, I'm going to school here."

Cathy gasped, "LooAnne Nash is going to school in my home town! Oh I just can't believe it! Where?"

"At the university."

"So am I!" Cathy exclaimed.

LooAnne was elated to hear this, for she wanted nothing more than someone at the college she knew. "Are you boarding at the college?" she asked.

Cathy shook her head, "My brother, sister, and I live downtown where he can be close to the bank so I walk to my classes. Are you staying at the dorm?"

"No I'm not either, my uncle arranged for me to stay at Belle Hall."

Cathy's eyes grew wide upon hearing the name of one of the greatest mansions in the city. "Belle Hall!" she exclaimed, "Oh that place is so beautiful!"

LooAnne smiled modestly, "I must admit I've never seen it. I've never really left Decatur before and this whole environment makes me rather nervous."

"Oh don't be nervous, Miss Nash. Everybody here is real nice." Cathy's eyes twinkled as she spoke, "And there are some real nice young men at school too."

At that moment the waiter stopped to take their order. LooAnne and Cathy decided to have the daily special and two iced teas. The waiter said that it was coming right up and then he strode away.

LooAnne sighed, "To be completely honest with you, I think I've had my full of nice young men."

"Had more than one have you?" Cathy smiled.

LooAnne shook her head, "No, just one. That's really why I'm here. We were engaged for three years and then he left me for my uncle's ward. He was just after money and could get her's before he could mine. I needed to get away so Uncle Ricky and I decided on school here in Dallas. I've had my full of young men, I never want to see another again," LooAnne stated bitterly.

"Oh not everyone's like this fortune hunter you're talking about," Cathy assured her.

"In my case I'm afraid they are. Every fella that ever looks at me has money on his mind and greed in his heart."

"Leave it to the Almighty, Miss Nash. There'll be some young fella out there to love you for you, I know it."

"Thank you," LooAnne smiled at Cathy's kind words. "I take it then that you have a suitor in mind?" she grinned.

Cathy shrugged, "I actually just broke it off with the fella I was courting. There wasn't anything wrong with him I just didn't like him in that way. It really crushed him, though. I really didn't know I'd hurt him that bad."

"Well my former fiancé knew how bad he would hurt me and he did it anyway. He never had loved me so I suppose I should be grateful that I didn't end up married to him but it's going to take a while to forget him I'm afraid."

"I know how you feel. But once that special someone comes along he'll steal your heart and you'll forget all about that scoundrel who tried to hurt you."

LooAnne looked dubiously at Cathy but smiled. "I hope you're right, Cathy."

"It's true," she insisted. "And I'm gonna make it my goal to find you another suitor. That is if you'll agree to be my friend?"

Immediately LooAnne's past experiences took precedence in her mind. She had been trained from birth not to trust anyone and no matter how she had worked to break this train of thought it was ingrained in her and she trusted no one but her uncle.

"Am I being too forward again?" Cathy asked. "My brother is always telling me I'm doing that."

"Oh no, Miss Morrison. You've been kinder to me than a lot of people, I'm just not experienced when it comes to friends."

"I understand; you're used to people who like you only for your money as you're fiance did."

LooAnne nodded, "It's hard to know a man's true intentions before it's too late."

Cathy nodded, "I know what you mean, when my brother first took over the bank that's the way it was with all the people I knew. It turned out they didn't want my friendship, they all wanted cheap loans. That's why I took to you first off, cause you're never gonna want a loan from my brother."

LooAnne laughed, feeling the reluctance drain away, "No, I suppose I'm not. And I'd be happy to be your friend, Miss Morrison, if you'll promise to give my over-cautiousness a chance."

Cathy smiled, "In that case you must call me Cathy."

"And you must call me LooAnne."

Cathy smiled a bright smile and the conversation went off in a different direction. After the girl's late lunch was over, Cathy paid the bill and then she grabbed her purse and LooAnne's suitcase and led the way through town toward the university. They were almost there when LooAnne caught sight of a man standing on the other side of the street watching both she and Cathy intently. He was leaning against a brick building, his muscular arms crossed over his broad chest. At first glance LooAnne was sure she knew him from somewhere. His dark features and toned body reminded LooAnne very much of someone she could not seem to place.

His narrow, almost black eyes locked with her's from beneath the brim of his hat and a mischievous grin slowly grew on his face as they stared at one another. LooAnne instantly looked away, trying to convince herself he was nothing more than a cowhand deprived of proper social skills, but all the while searching the back of her mind, wondering how she knew this mysterious man and why he had looked at her so strangely.

TWO

Belle Hall

Upon arriving at the university Cathy gave LooAnne an extensive tour of the grounds, showing her where all her classes would be held. They walked about the school grounds until LooAnne realized that it was growing very late in the afternoon. She still had to get settled at Belle Hall and was sure that the house keeper was wondering what delayed her arrival.

"I had better go get settled in before the housekeeper grows worried and contacts my uncle," LooAnne told Cathy as they neared the library.

"Alright," Cathy agreed. "I'll walk you there since it's on the way to my brother's bank."

LooAnne thanked her and the two made their way down the sidewalks in the direction of downtown Dallas.

The city was much larger than Decatur and home to many factories and large businesses. People milled about the streets and new and old automobiles rattled down the road with the occasional horse drawn carriage. But there was still the familiar smells of food and merchandise mingling with the friendly chatter that reminded her of home and caused her to smile. LooAnne drew many curious looks from passersby who recognized her from newspapers and magazine articles. She was used to the stares from her own townspeople, men and woman whom she mostly knew and associated with on occasion, but these people were strangers to her and yet they knew her name and the names of her family. LooAnne had expected such but found their stares much more unsettling then she imagined. She could not wait to get within the privacy of Belle Hall, the former home of her uncle's late grandmother. Ricky had told her that the house was one of the first purchased by the Nash's after making their fortune off the California Gold Rush many years before he was born. He had not told her much about the house it's self but of its occupants. He had said that only caretakers had lived there since the death of his grandmother almost thirty years before. Ricky assured his niece that they were all very amiable people who would welcome her with open arms.

LooAnne only hoped that this was true as she and Cathy grew closer and closer to the great house.

When they rounded the corner LooAnne gasped as she stared in awe at the structure. Surrounded by many beautiful homes Belle Hall stood back from the road, guarded by a wrought iron gate adorned with intricate design. The house itself was shaded by cypress trees and a stone walkway led to the front entrance lined with flowering bushes and dogwoods. Four white columns in Corinthian order boldly defined the front porch, supporting the roof overhead where men could be seen trimming tree branches away from the building's edge. The house was a marble white with intricate trim about the roof and window panes.

"Isn't it beautiful?" Cathy asked LooAnne in awe.
She nodded, still staring at this mansion which her uncle
had given her to live in for the next few years. It was
indeed one of the most beautiful houses LooAnne had ever
seen. She knew that her uncle owned many large estates
but he often mentioned this one when talking of his
favorites and LooAnne was anxious to see the inside.
She and Cathy approached the iron gate which had a large
plaque welded on its front with the inscription:

Belle Hall
Private Property of R.W. Nash

"Is it locked?" Cathy asked as LooAnne looked over the
engraving and then at the gate itself.
She reached out and gave it a forceful push, causing the
gate to open instantly, creaking on its hinges as it swung
inward.
LooAnne looked back at Cathy and said, "Well, I suppose
we can go in. Are you coming?"
Cathy nodded and the two tentatively stepped through the
gate and onto the stone walkway which led to the house.
LooAnne pushed the gate to close it and both girls jumped
slightly as it clanged shut. They slowly made their way up
the path to the front entrance of the house, pausing
momentarily to gaze upward at its marble walls which
towered over their heads. Both girls then climbed the
marble stairs to the front door, taking in the intricacy of
the columns and door frame.
LooAnne and Cathy looked at one another in uncertainty,
then back at the iron door.

"Go ahead, knock," Cathy urged. "It is your uncle's house after all, and you said that the housekeeper is expecting you."

LooAnne nodded and swallowed her nerves before lifting the brass knocker and letting it fall with a clang against the door. The girls did not wait long before they heard the door being unlocked and it swung open revealing a tall man with thin features whom LooAnne assumed to be the butler. He did not open the door wide, only enough to stand in the gap between the girls and the front hall. He peered at them over his thin-rimmed glasses before his eyes rested on LooAnne's face, causing his posture to straighten instantly.

"You're Miss LooAnne Nash if I'm not mistaken?" he asked, his baritone taking them by surprise.

LooAnne nodded, "Yes I am. My uncle said that I was expected."

The butler nodded and stood back, opening the door wide to let LooAnne and Cathy through. They walked in and immediately drew in their breath as they took in the beauty of the house's interior. The entry hall was very large, adorned with small trinkets and old pictures of Nash forefathers. A thick red carpet covered both the entry hall and the wide staircase which wound its way to the second floor. A silver chandelier, sparkling with polished crystals hung from the ceiling in the center of the room, casting a patterned light on the beige colored walls.

LooAnne heard Cathy gasp quietly as her eyes scanned the beauty of the hall, taking in every detail carefully.

LooAnne looked for only a moment before her attention was taken by the butler who told her that the housekeeper was indeed expecting them and that he would go fetch her.

LooAnne thanked him and then watched as he briskly walked down the hall towards the back of the house.

"Oh LooAnne," Cathy breathed, still in awe. "It's so beautiful!"

LooAnne nodded, "It most certainly is."

"Did Mr. Nash ever live here?"

LooAnne shook her head, "No he's lived at the Nash Estate all of his life." A small smile tugged at the corner of LooAnne's mouth as she thought of her uncle's reasons for staying in Decatur. "It's his home," she stated. "He could never leave the place he was raised or the people he's grown so close to."

Cathy nodded understandingly. "I don't blame him, but this place is just down right spectacular!"

"It really is. I wonder what the upstairs looks like?"

"You'll not have to wait long to see it, Miss Nash," came an unfamiliar voice from down the hall.

Both Cathy and LooAnne looked in the direction of the cheerful proclamation and saw a middle-aged woman walking towards them. She had her slightly graying hair hidden beneath a cap and her long soft blue skirt barely touching the floor. Her blouse was adorned with a broach and beaded belt, giving her the perfect posture.

She smiled kindly at both LooAnne and Cathy. "It's an honor to have you here, Miss Nash. I'm Mrs. Andrews, the housekeeper."

"It's very nice to meet you, Mrs. Andrews. This is my friend Cathy Morrison."

"Ah yes, your brother runs the downtown bank, am I right?"

Cathy nodded and shook Mrs. Andrews' hand. "Yes ma-am, he does. I hope it's alright that I came with LooAnne?

She didn't know where the house was so I'm showing her around town."

"Of course that's perfectly fine," Mrs. Andrews assured her. "Any friend of Miss Nash's is always welcome here." Cathy thanked her as the butler reappeared in the hall and smiled kindly at the girls.

"Ladies, this is my husband, Matt Andrews," the kindly lady smiled. "Miss Nash, he'll take your bags for you."

"It's nice to meet you, ma-am," he bowed slightly and then took LooAnne's bags.

"If you like I'll show you to your room, Miss Nash?" Mrs. Andrews offered.

LooAnne smiled and nodded, "Yes thank you." She and Cathy followed the couple up the grand staircase to be met with another long hallway, carpeted with the same thick, red carpet. It was lined with closed doors on one side and a small seating area on the other, as well as a balcony where you could look down on the entryway.

Mrs. Andrews walked down the hall and entered the room at the very end. Her husband set the bags at the foot of the king sized bed and then left the room as his wife showed LooAnne its interior. There was a fireplace with two embroidered arm chairs on either side of it, and at the far end of the room was a small round table with an arrangement of flowers as centerpiece. Beyond that was the bureau and a long mirror positioned beside the closets. The high posted bed sat directly across from the bathroom door, piled high with feather pillows and a floral comforter. It was large yet still very cozy which LooAnne found much to her liking. "It's very lovely, Mrs. Andrews," she smiled. "Thank you for all the trouble you've gone to for me."

"Oh my land, it's been no trouble at all, Miss Nash. The way your uncle talked about you made all the staff quite anxious to have you come visit. I'll let you get settled in and send up your maid. Her name is Clara and she happens to be my second oldest. She's a very sweet girl and I hope you will get along."

"Oh I'm sure we will."

"And I hope you don't mind if my youngest boys come and go? They're seventeen and fourteen and are supposed to stay in the servant's quarters when they're outta school, they shouldn't be in the way."

"Oh of course I don't mind," LooAnne assured her, "thank you again, Mrs. Andrews."

"No need to thank me. And Miss Morrison you stay as long as you like."

Cathy smiled and she too thanked the housekeeper before she disappeared out the door. The moment it was shut Cathy let out a girlish squeal, "Oh LooAnne it's so beautiful! My brother will never believe me when I tell him I got to go inside Belle Hall!"

LooAnne laughed. "It is very lovely isn't it."

"Is it much like the Nash Estate?"

LooAnne frowned slightly and shook her head. "I'll have to admit it's not. The Nash Estate is a bit smaller and very homey. This place is lovely but it's so big and imposing."

"And you like the estate better I'm supposing?"

LooAnne nodded and shrugged, "It's home. As I said, I had never left it until my uncle insisted upon school here in Dallas."

"Do you wish you hadn't come?" Cathy asked hesitantly.

LooAnne shook her head. "No, I just wish there had been a college in Decatur where I could have stayed at home.

But since there's not I'll make the best of it."

Just then there was a light knock on the bedroom door before it was opened to reveal a young woman who looked to be in her early twenties. She wore a maid's uniform with her light blond hair rolled at the crown of her head; she wore the same sweet smile and kind eyes as her mother.

"You must be Clara?" LooAnne asked.

The young maid nodded, "Yes ma-am. If you need anything, please don't hesitate to ask."

LooAnne returned Clara's kind smile and thanked her before the maid began unpacking LooAnne's bags.

"Well, I suppose I'd better be off," Cathy said. "My younger sister should be getting home from school soon."

LooAnne nodded understandingly. "Thank you so much for welcoming me as you did. I would be quite lonely and probably lost if it weren't for you."

Cathy shook her head, waving off the compliment. "It was nothing. I'm glad to have found a new friend. You should come to church services with us tomorrow."

LooAnne agreed to meeting her new found friends the next morning for church. She and Cathy embraced before the latter left Belle Hall, leaving LooAnne to her unpacking.

THREE

Voices in the Night

LooAnne had successfully unpacked all her belongings and had a brief conversation with her uncle over the telephone in the entry hall. He had been very glad to know she was settled at Belle Hall. Though he had not expressed it himself, LooAnne detected a hint of loneliness in his voice. This had been what she most feared when leaving. Her uncle had no close family but her; his brother, Robert, lived in southern Texas with his family quite a few miles away and all Ricky's other relations were scattered across the western plains.

The thought of her uncle being lonely weighed on her mind as LooAnne lay on the grand bed staring at the small fire Clara had lit due to the chill in the room. The house was very quiet and though it was nothing less than beautiful, it was not LooAnne's home, and it housed no one but her and the staff, whom she knew very little. The crackle of the fire and the warmth it produced caused a drowsiness to come over LooAnne who was tired from her long journey. She closed her eyes with the intention of resting the short time until dinner was served but she unintentionally fell into a deep sleep.

When LooAnne's eyes finally opened she was surprised to find herself in the dark with only a small glow from the fire. LooAnne sat up and rubbed her eyes then squinted at the clock only to see that it was going on midnight! LooAnne frowned, having not intended on sleeping for so long.

"Now I'll never go back to sleep," she mumbled to herself as she quietly got out of bed. She straightened her day suit and then approached the fire with the intention of stirring the coals. She reached for the poker and was about to take hold of it when her ears detected the muffled thud of the door downstairs!

LooAnne froze, listening intently for any following sounds, but she heard nothing. Leaving the dying fire, she strode quietly to the bedroom door and slowly cracked it open. It was then that the sound of voices reached her ears; whispers coming from the first floor. She could not distinguish the source nor what was being said so LooAnne opened the door wide enough for her slim figure to slip through and into the hallway where she could see a small glow of light coming from the entry hall downstairs! LooAnne silently closed her bedroom door and tiptoed down the carpeted hall where she could look down at the front entrance. She stayed close within the shadows, careful not to be detected by whoever stood below her. The dim light of a hall lamp could be seen next to the grand iron door but it gave off too little light for LooAnne to distinguish the faces that stood around it.

As she grew closer she saw that there were only two beings talking in very low whispers. She made it to the top of the stairs and squinted to get a better look at the two.

One, she now saw, was taller than the other and had very broad shoulders that cast a vast shadow on the wall. The other was the petite frame of a woman, she being the one who was whispering.

The couple did not move as they quietly conversed in the front of the hall. LooAnne disliked the thought of eavesdropping but this was, after all, her uncle's house, and should something nefarious be taking place in the wee hours of night, she would need to know.

LooAnne quietly crept down the stairs and slowly the voices began to grow louder and more clear. She could now distinguish Clara's soft whispers and she was intrigued even further as she thought of her innocent young maid meeting a man at midnight. Surely this was something she needed to confront! Clara could not let men into the house after daylight, and certainly not without the knowledge of her parents.

LooAnne straightened from her crouched position on the stairs and walked down them more boldly then before, approaching the couple as quietly as she could so the man would not have time to flee, if that should be his intention, before she could see his face.

"It's dangerous for you to be here," Clara's words were now audible and LooAnne clearly heard the man's reply as she neared them.

"I know it is but I can't see you during the day, they're still looking for me," his voice was low like a mans and yet young as though he were still in his youth.

"I still don't understand why you can't tell the police about these men. I know my brother would do something about it."

"Your brother is a right kind fella, but I told you I can't go to him. I can't go to no lawmen."

"Why, Stephen? What has you so afraid of people who could help you?"

The young man, whose face LooAnne could not see in the dark, shook his head. "You wouldn't understand, Clara. No one would."

"Have you done something wrong?"

"No!" he cried. "I swear I ain't done nothin' wrong."

LooAnne took this chance to make her presence known. "Then why are you afraid of the law?"

Clara and her young companion whirled around to face LooAnne, both of them obviously startled.

"Miss Nash!" Clara cried but before LooAnne could say anything the young man turned and yanked open the iron door, running through it onto the grounds!

"Stephen, come back!" Clara called after him but he paid her no mind and dashed through the gate out of sight, but not before LooAnne caught a glimpse of his face in the streetlamp. From what she had seen he was indeed a youth with very broad shoulders and what she thought had been a wisp of ginger-red hair protruding from beneath his worn hat.

"Clara who was he?" LooAnne demanded, turning to the young maid who looked extremely frightened and on edge.

"I – I..." Clara looked back and forth between LooAnne and the open front door, seeming extremely conflicted.

"Clara, tell me this instant or I'll have to fetch your father!" LooAnne continued to pressure the girl.

"No, please!" she begged, the light from the candle beginning to reflect off the tears that were gathering in her eyes. "You can't tell him! Please, Miss Nash!"

LooAnne's eyes softened upon seeing how frightened the

maid was but she could not make light of the situation. "Clara, do you know how dangerous it is to let a strange man in the house at night without the knowledge of anyone, and you being a single young woman at that. Surely you must know the indecency of such a thing." Clara nodded and looked down shamefully. "Please forgive me, Miss Nash. I promise you he had nothing but honorable intentions."

"Even so, it is very dangerous to allow mere acquaintances access to such a grand house holding valuable possessions, not to mention without the consent of the owner. And this man all but admitted his dislike for the law, surely you see the reasons for my concern?"

Clara nodded and sniffled a bit, "I do, Miss Nash. I don't blame you for being angry but I promise I didn't mean any harm."

LooAnne sighed, lowering her voice an octave. "I know you didn't, but this kind of thing can't be taken lightly. It's not only dangerous to the house and to its occupants, but to you as well. To be alone at night with a man who could do whatever he pleased to any of us without you having the power to stop him."

"I know the risks, ma-am, but I promise you he would never do anything wrong."

"Who is *he*?" LooAnne asked again.

Clara sighed as if defeated and said, "His name is Stephen Parker. He..." Clara trailed off.

"He what, Clara?" LooAnne probed.

"He – he – he's my fiancé," she said quickly, her voice growing quiet as she confessed her secret.

LooAnne was very surprised at this revelation. "Fiance?" she cried a bit too loudly for Clara instantly begged her not to awaken the rest of the house.

"If my father finds out there's no telling what he'll do!"

"If this man is as honorable as you say then why does your father not know of your engagement?" LooAnne asked.

"Well – I – I can't tell you, Miss Nash."

LooAnne raised her eyebrows at the maid. "Forgive me for speaking plainly, Clara, but you just let a man into a house that I'm staying in, owned by my uncle without my consent and under the nose of your father. I'm afraid if you don't tell me what's going on I'll have to either inform Mr. Andrews or find someone to take your place."

"No, you can't fire me!" Clara cried, turning her tearful eyes on LooAnne pleadingly.

"Believe me, I don't want to," LooAnne assured her. "But you have to tell me who that young man is so that I know he's not a threat to the people in this house." LooAnne tried her best to confront the situation as her uncle would have, with firmness and understanding.

Clara thought about it for a moment before she sighed and looked again to the carpeted floor. "Alright," she whispered in defeat. "Can we talk where we're sure no one's gonna hear?"

LooAnne nodded; she pulled the front door closed, made sure it was locked tightly, and then led the way up to her room where the fire had already died, leaving the room in complete darkness.

"I'll start the fire again if you want, Miss Nash," Clara said as LooAnne turned on one of the lamps.

"No, it's fine, I'm anxious to hear what you have to say. Sit down," LooAnne gestured to one of the armchairs in front of the fireplace and Clara reluctantly took a seat.

LooAnne took the one directly across from it and looked

at her maid questioningly, waiting for her to begin.
Clara looked down at her lap, playing with her hands nervously. "I guess it started about this time last year," she began. "One of the house cooks had sent me to run errands. I had just left the grocery and was walking back here with two very large bags in my arms. I couldn't see all that well around them and the next thing I knew I had accidentally bumped shoulders with someone and dropped all my groceries on the sidewalk. I started apologizing like crazy and went to pick up my things but the man I had run into grabbed me and started yelling at me for being in the way. He was screaming in my face and drawing a lot of attention. I tried to pull my arm away from him but that just made him hold tighter.

"I was right scared and thought he was gonna hit me but then suddenly this fella shoved the guy away from me and started yelling at him. I was so disoriented I didn't know what he was saying, it did seem like they knew each other though, the way they were yelling back and forth. Eventually the man who had grabbed me hit the other man in the mouth and they started throwing punches at each other.

My older brother, Peter, who's a deputy, came running and tried to separate the two of them but they both ran off and Peter was too worried about me to chase after them. He got me home safe and after that I didn't see either of the men again until about a month later. I was walking home from church one morning and suddenly a man walked up next to me and tipped his hat. I instantly recognized him as the man who had saved me and he introduced himself as Stephen Parker. I, of course, told him how thankful I was to him and he said it was nothing but begged me not to tell anyone about him when I asked him to come meet my parents. Since he had done so much for me I figured it was the least I could do in return so I didn't say anything. We met at least once a week after that and then once a week became twice and then before I knew it we were seeing each other nearly every day." Clara took a deep breath and continued, staring into the dark fireplace, going over the past events in her mind. The next memory made a small smile tug at the corner of her lips. "I must admit that I had never had my eyes on young men until Stephen came along," she whispered. "But as time went by I slowly fell in love with him and him with me. He asked me to be his wife last week and I accepted." She then looked up at LooAnne, her eyes not tearful but dancing with happiness. "I've never loved or cared for anyone as much as I love and care for Stephen, Miss Nash. I feel as though nothing can separate us, as though nothing could ever go wrong – but..." Clara paused, her face clouding as she looked at LooAnne who had listened intently through the story. "But there's something holding him back. Some reason we have to sneak around to see each other, some reason he's always looking over his shoulder. All he tells me is that there's some men after him and he's not safe."

That was the point where LooAnne broke her silence. "Men after him?" she asked. "Does he say who?"

Clara shook her head. "No, he won't tell me. He won't tell me a lot o' things. Says it's not safe for me to know."

LooAnne pondered this for a moment before laying a gentle hand on Clara's shoulder causing the young maid to look up at her. "I know you're not going to like me saying this, Clara, but are you sure it's not the authorities he's running from? Maybe he did something in the past that -"

"No!" Clara exclaimed, withdrawing from LooAnne's comforting hand. "Stephen is the sweetest, gentlest, most honorable man I've ever met. He would never do anything to get himself in trouble with the law."

"But can you be sure of that?" LooAnne persisted. "You said yourself he seemed to know that man who grabbed you on the street. If he keeps such company, then the real him might not be the upright man he shows to you."

Clara shook her head vigorously. "No, Miss Nash, I refuse to believe it! Not once during our relationship have I seen that man or anyone like him. Stephen is nothing but good and kind to everyone he meets!"

"You say that you've been sneaking around with him for almost a year now. What do you do when you're together?" LooAnne questioned wondering where this young man took Clara when they were in each other's company.

"Well, on week days when I go to run errands he meets me just down the road and goes with me sometimes. Every Sunday I tell my parents I'm going on a walk or something and he and I walk for hours down the country roads just outside the city. He's staying at the inn on the other side of town and sometimes we sit on the porch swing and talk. The land lady knows me and she lets me stay for supper sometimes."

"But he has no permanent residence?" LooAnne asked. Clara shook her head. "He has no family and came here in search of a job. At first he did odd jobs for his landlady, keeping her house up in return for his room and board but now he works at the mills. He spends most of his time over there."

LooAnne nodded, "And why was he here tonight?" she

asked, detecting a flicker of uncertainty in her maid's eyes upon hearing this question.

"Um – he just wanted to see me," Clara answered after a brief moment.

LooAnne leaned down and looked Clara in the eyes, "I know you're lying. Tell me the truth," she ordered though with a gentle tone.

"Um – well – he," Clara sighed and finished, "he wants me to run away with him to be married...tomorrow night." LooAnne sat back in her chair, surprised that this man who Clara spoke so highly of was asking her to leave her family without any goodbye and run away with him to who knows where. He was obviously hiding something and wanted to ensnare Clara before she found out by marrying her.

"Miss Nash, it's not what you think!" Clara came to his defense upon seeing LooAnne's somewhat appalled expression. "That wasn't all he said. He told me that those men were getting closer and he had to leave but couldn't bear to leave me here not knowing when he would return."

"Clara do you not see the danger you're putting yourself in?" LooAnne asked. "He's admitted to being chased by some men but he's told you nothing else on the matter and now he wants you to marry and join him in a life of running from something you have no knowledge of! You don't know what kind of life he will offer you, you don't know of his background, and you don't know why he's being 'chased' by these 'men'."

Clara got to her feet and turned away from LooAnne as if to hide from the truth in her words. "But I know he loves me, Miss Nash," Clara whispered, her voice cracking. "And I know I love him. Is that not all I need to know to become his wife?"

It was this sentence that struck LooAnne like a blow to the face. Reality of who she was, of what she was, and of whom she had been born surfaced from where she had hidden it deep within her. Had her mother not done the same thing Clara wanted to with the same reasoning? Had Amanda Nash not left all of her family to worry for her because she had loved Jason Luther? Had that not been the reason LooAnne was here now, hiding her true identity under the name and protection of her illustrious uncle as she had been for six years?

This thought rendered LooAnne wordless as she realized she was fighting a fight her uncle had once fought the night his sister had left.

"Miss Nash?" LooAnne heard Clara sniffle and this brought her out of her deep thoughts and she realized the young maid was now facing her with curious, watery eyes. "Are you alright, ma-am? I didn't mean to -"

"No no, Clara," LooAnne whispered reassuringly, smiling warmly at the girl to mask her inward pain. "You've not said anything to upset me. I just want you to see what a risk your taking, not only for yourself but for your children." As LooAnne spoke she thought of herself and of her brothers who were forever tainted by her mother's choices, their minds molded into the evil ways of the people who had raised them. She remembered well the hurt on her mother's face when her oldest sons would return from a raid and brag of the things they had stolen and the people they killed in cold blood. Though she had no reason to think this Stephen fellow to be anything as bad as a Luther, she did not want anything at all similar for Clara.

"You've got every right to marry the man you love and to take on whatever life he is offering you, but when you do please remember, you're taking it on for your children as well. They will look to you for protection and you more than any human alive will be the one that must give them that, even before they're born."

Clara looked at LooAnne thoughtfully, her eyes still shining with tears. "Please tell me what to do, Miss Nash?" she begged, her voice thick with emotion. "I love him so much but what you said is very true."

LooAnne gave Clara a sympathetic look and said, "If he's the right one for you, the Almighty will make a way for the both of you but that might mean you wait until his situation is different. If you truly love him the way you say and he loves you the way he says, then you will both gladly wait as long as you must for each other. I don't know who the man I'm supposed to spend the rest of my life with is, but if he's out there I'll wait a thousand years for him."

By this time a tear had escaped Clara's eye and rolled down her cheek. She smiled and embraced LooAnne in a hug as she rose from her seat. "Thank you, Miss Nash. Thank you for everything."

LooAnne smiled, somewhat relieved. "You've very welcome, Clara. Now let's both get back to bed. I see no need in telling anyone about tonight's events, but you need to make things right with this man of yours. If he decides not to wait for you then he's not worth it."

Clara nodded, pulling away from LooAnne and starting for the door. "I'll make things right with him, Miss Nash. You don't know how thankful I am for all you've said."

"Your very welcome, Clara."

The young maid turned and closed the door, leaving LooAnne standing alone in her large bedroom, praying that things would turn out well for Clara, and that Stephen Parker was not as dangerous as he sounded.

FOUR

First Encounter

LooAnne slept little through the remainder of the night. Her mind whirling as it replayed the events of the past hours. She had not been in Dallas a full day and already it was proving to be much more than the supposed dullness of school and studies. She yearned to talk to her uncle of the night's happenings but she had promised Clara secrecy and could not betray her confidence.

LooAnne found herself drifting off in early morning only to be awakened a few hours later by a light knocking on her door. She sat up and rubbed the sleep from her eyes before calling, "Who is it?"

"It's Clara, Miss Nash," came the young maid's soft voice. "Come in," LooAnne answered as she looked at the clock only to see that she had, again, slept beyond her intended time. It was already seven thirty, meaning church was soon to start and LooAnne had promised Cathy to meet her outside Belle Hall.

LooAnne leaped from beneath the sheets as Clara entered, carrying LooAnne's already pressed Sunday dress in one hand whole balancing a tray of breakfast on the other.

"Oh Clara, you're a life saver!" LooAnne exclaimed as she relieved the young maid of her tray.

Clara smiled, "I'm sorry to wake you, Miss Nash."

"Oh no you're perfectly right to wake me," LooAnne assured. "I told Cathy I would go with her to service this morning and I'm still in my night clothes!"

"You eat while I get your things together then I'll help you get ready," Clara offered. She laid the floral silk dress on the bed as LooAnne began devouring her breakfast.

Once she had finished Clara helped her into her dress and then un-boxed LooAnne's Panama hat, handing it to her before donning her shoes and gloves. Once LooAnne was fully dressed and presentable she thanked Clara and hurried downstairs where Mrs. Andrews was just walking by.

"Ah Miss Nash, I hope you slept well?" she asked kindly. LooAnne nodded having no intention of telling Clara's mother all that had happened that night. "Yes, Mrs. Andrews the bed is very comfy. Thank you."

"Oh you're most welcome. The chauffeur will have the sedan around immediately."

"Oh no thank you, Mrs. Andrews. I told Cathy I would meet her and Bill outside. It's such a lovely day I believe we'll just walk."

"Well in that case, we'll see you at services, Miss Nash. Please be careful, dear."

LooAnne smiled and nodded, "I will, Mrs. Andrews." LooAnne went outside the grand house and down the stone drive to the iron gate, admiring the beautiful morning. She slipped through the iron bars and looked up and down the street in search of Cathy and her brother but failed to see them. LooAnne sighed and decided she had no other recourse but to wait since she didn't know how to find the church.

As she stood her eyes began to wander down the tree shaded road lined with colonial homes and two other grand estates. This was where the most prestigious individuals of the city lived, not too far from the center of town. LooAnne decided to walk down the road, hoping to meet her company as she did. LooAnne could not help but take in the beauty of the day as she leisurely walked; for late September it was quite warm and she enjoyed the slight breeze that was blowing down the nearly abandoned street. It was not long before LooAnne reached the crossroads which led to the town square. Automobiles and the occasional horse drawn carriage passed her by, along with a few people on foot who nodded to her politely, but LooAnne still failed to see either Cathy or Bill and this was beginning to worry her. She decided to turn back and walk with the Andrews', coming to the conclusion that Cathy had either forgotten or for some reason could not come. LooAnne turned to start back but froze a moment later and inhale a breath as she caught sight of a man standing only a few feet down the road. His tall figure was leaned against a Fringe tree, his fingers masterfully flipping a small pocket knife about in his palm. Chills ran down LooAnne's spine as she realized who he was. It was the same man she had seen the day before, and he was watching her...again!

Their eyes locked and the same mischievous grin from their previous encounter crossed his face, causing LooAnne's body to stiffen slightly. She knew him, she was sure she did, but she still could not think why. Her first instinct told her to head back to the known safety of Belle

Hall, but the man stood between her and the grand estate. LooAnne was not about to cross his path but she had very little knowledge of the city's layout. Seeing no other alternative she decided to cross the street and then pass him on the other side with what she hoped was little mishap.

LooAnne stepped out into the street and strode across towards the opposite sidewalk. Upon reaching it she glanced back over her shoulder and what she saw caused her heart to race. The man had moved from his position beneath the Fringe tree and was now making his way across the street towards her, knife in hand!

LooAnne tried to contain her sense of panic as her stride quickened in desperation to get to safety. She could see the iron fence that surrounded Belle Hall and its heavy gate offering her protection from the sly character who perused her, if she could only reach it!

With the quickening of LooAnne's strides the man's pace also increased until the two were almost at a run. As the distance between them lessened LooAnne decided to make a mad dash for the hall only to find that she was greatly restricted by the floral silk skirt of her Sunday dress! She fumbled to grab it up in an effort to free her legs but just as she did LooAnne felt the gruff, calloused hands of her pursuer take hold of her arm and yank her to a stop! She gasped and instantly began to struggle against the stranger's hold, using every technique she had ever been taught to free herself but each action was met as if this man had been prepared for any move she might use to evade him.

"Quit your strugglin' or it'll be worse for ya!" the man's gruff voice commanded as he restrained her hands and placed the knife against her throat!

LooAnne's mind whirled as adrenaline pulsed through her body! The man's voice sounded so familiar, as though she had heard its gruff baritone before, but still she could not withdraw the exact memory from the back of her mind as it fogged over with panic, knowing that she was helpless against this man! With his prisoner restrained under the threat of his knife the man began to drag her behind one of the large homes which looked to be unoccupied! Despite her fear of being cut LooAnne began to scream and call out for help, hoping and praying that Cathy and her brother Bill were not far! But no one came and her screams only angered the man who roughly clapped one of his calloused hands over her mouth, muffling her desperate calls as he pressed the knife closer!

"If you ever wanna be seen alive again I suggest you keep your mouth shut!" he hissed in her ear as he drug her down the side of the abandoned house.

LooAnne could feel her heart sinking as they grew further and further out of sight. Fear of being taken away by her kidnapper caused a knot to form in her chest. Why was he doing this? What did he want with her? Why had he been watching her ever since she arrived on the noon train? And above all, what was he planning to do to her?

These thoughts had LooAnne's mind racing. She hated the feeling of being at anyone's mercy, of being helpless against any person or persons. She was beginning to lose hope of freeing herself when a low, commanding voice cut through the air, startling both LooAnne and her captor.

"What do you think you're doin'?"

LooAnne's abductor whirled around and that was when she saw him; the man who had come to her rescue.

He was tall and muscular, broad and clean cut, the perfect image of rugged masculinity. His complexion was dark from the Texas sun in great contrast to his sandy blond hair. He wore a dark brown Sunday suit that looked to be quite worn but still presentable and matched the felt of his Stetson on which was printed the star of a Deputy Sheriff! LooAnne felt relief rush through her body as she locked her gaze on the lawman, silently pleaded with him to help her. His light blue eyes narrowed as they moved from LooAnne to the man who was trying to abduct her.

"Let her go, mister," he commanded, his Texan drawl implying a threat if the man did not comply.

LooAnne felt the stranger chuckle. "What are you gonna do about it, Deputy?" he countered.

The young lawman threw back his suit coat revealing a holstered Colt 38 that shone in the morning sunlight. "You let her go or I'll take her myself," he demanded, laying a warning hand on his sidearm.

The man, however, seemed undaunted as he huffed in defiance. "You fire that gun and the bullet will have to go through her first! Now you get back to mindin' your own business and maybe Miss Nash here won't have to die." LooAnne felt her heart begin to speed again as she realized she must do something to get out of the line of fire. Hoping beyond hope that the deputy would react accordingly, LooAnne took advantage of the man's distracted mind and yanked her arm free of his loosening hold. Before he could react she drug her elbow deep into the center of his stomach knocking the breath out of him and causing his arms to release her as they withdrew to clutch his middle, his sharp weapon falling to the ground! LooAnne tried to jump away from him but did not expect his instant recovery as he lunged forward in a desperate attempt to grab her! One of his large hands took hold of her upper arm and was about to yank her back when suddenly his grip loosened as his body was thrown to the ground! LooAnne stumbled away from him and gasped as she witnessed the young deputy attempt to pin the man to the ground, but the stranger was large and extremely muscular. He took a swing at the deputy's jaw, connecting his fist with such force that the young lawman was thrown back onto the ground. Instead of tackling him as LooAnne assumed the rogue would do he turned and made a grab for her! LooAnne jumped to escape his hold but tripped over an unseen garden tool and fell backwards onto the lawn with her potential abductor only inches away!

He reached down and seized LooAnne by her wrist, yanking her roughly to her feet as she fought to get away. "Let me go!" LooAnne cried, twisting her wrist to try and free it.

Her abductor looked beyond angry, her struggles only arousing his ire all the more. He raised his free hand and was about to bring it down across her face when it was grabbed from behind by the deputy! He yanked the man's arm back, causing him to fall away from LooAnne as both men toppled to the ground in a rage of fisticuffs!

The deputy was slightly dazed from the previous blow but he struck the man's jaw angrily, determined to overpower him. His opponent however was a skilled fighter and delivered punch after punch to the lawman's face and stomach.

LooAnne stood to the side watching anxiously and praying that the deputy would prevail. But as the fight continued she realized that he was weakening as his punches did

little to deter the goon who by now had the upper hand.
With every blow he received the deputy grew weaker and
weaker. LooAnne knew she had to do something to help
him so she searched the yard desperately for a weapon.
Her eyes scanned the lawn only for a moment until they
landed on the gardening tool which she had tripped over
only moments before. A hoe! LooAnne grabbed it and
turned towards the altercation behind her. Her abductor
had the deputy pinned to the ground and was delivering
blows to his face as the deputy fought desperately to free
himself.

LooAnne raised the hoe and brought it down as hard she
could on the stranger's head! He let out a grunt and threw
his hands over his bleeding scalp, sinking to the ground
next to the deputy. LooAnne waited a moment to make
sure he was unconscious before she knelt next to her dazed
rescuer.

He tried to sit up but groaned and held his head in his
hands as it began to pulse with a throbbing pain.

"Lay back down," LooAnne commanded as she gently
eased his shoulders back against the grass.

"I – I'm okay," the young deputy tried to protest but
instinctively sank back, resting his bleeding head on the
ground, his eyes closed against the stinging pain in his
face. LooAnne pulled his hand away to examine the
damage and found many bruising welts on his forehead
and cheek bones, matting his hairline down with a crimson
red liquid. His nose was bleeding and his lips were both
cut.

"We need to get you to a doctor, Deputy," LooAnne said,
her voice still a bit shaky. "You need stitches
immediately."

"I – I'll be – fine," the deputy croaked. He opened his eyes and looked up at LooAnne, staring into her's for only a moment before he tried once again to sit up.

"Easy," LooAnne warned as she took hold of his arm and helped him into a sitting position, all the while keeping a close eye on the unconscious man to her left.

The young deputy groaned and laid his head in his hands, waiting for the scenery around him to stop spinning.

"Are – are you alright?" his low voice asked as he looked up at her questioningly.

LooAnne nodded, "I'm perfectly fine, thanks to you."

The deputy tried to smile but winced as it pulled on his cut lip. "Just – just doin' my job, ma-am."

"What hurts the worst?" LooAnne asked, trying to evaluate the situation.

The deputy winced again as the pain was brought back to his mind. "My head," he answered, pressing his hand harder against it as if to push out the throbbing.

LooAnne was at a loss to know what to do. If the deputy was able to walk, she was sure she could assist him to Belle Hall, but that meant leaving behind the man who had tried to kidnap her. If he came to he might get away before they could come back, and he would be free to try again. LooAnne was already unsure that he would not regain consciousness any moment and was torn between the need to get the young lawman help and the new found fear of the man who lay to their side.

She finally decided that getting the deputy to a doctor took priority, especially after he had already saved her life.

"Do you think you can stand, Deputy..."

"Andrews," was the familiar name that the young man spoke, "Peter Andrews."

LooAnne was surprised upon hearing the name of the family that had made her feel so welcome at Belle Hall. And then it hit her! This was the brother whom Clara had spoken of when telling the story of how she had first met her supposed suitor. This was the oldest son of the housekeeper and butler at Belle Hall!

"You- you recognize the name," the young man presumed, glancing up at her slightly as the throbbing in his head eased a bit.

LooAnne smiled and nodded, "I do indeed, I suppose you already know mine?"

Peter Andrews nodded slightly, "My sister's told me about you."

LooAnne smiled, "I'm growing very fond of your sister, she's a very sweet girl. Now if we can get you to Belle Hall then maybe your father will come and take charge of that hooligan before he comes to?"

Peter Andrews nodded in agreement and LooAnne took his arm and slowly helped him to his feet. She steadied him as he swayed and felt his hand gently grip her arm. "Are you alright?" she asked.

He blinked for a moment, making no move to walk, but eventually nodded and took a slow step forward, leaning on LooAnne for balance.

Gradually they made their way out to the street, where the gates of Belle Hall were only a few yards away.

LooAnne began to wonder what had happened to Cathy and her brother. She was sure they would have been there by now but there was still no sign of them.

LooAnne saw Peter Andrews' automobile just down the road, a golden star on the side of it reading, **Dallas Co. Sheriff.** She was so thankful that he had come along; had he not she was sure to still be in the hands of the man whose intentions were unknown. This brought on another train of thought as LooAnne wondered what the man had wanted and why he had tried to take her to begin with? But the only way to know for sure was to get a confession out of him and that would only be possible should he still be there when Mr. Andrews went to get him.

The two were about half way there when the voice of a young boy reached their ears. "Peter!" he exclaimed in surprise.

Both LooAnne and the deputy looked up and found a boy, in his early youth, who had just come from within the grounds, dressed in his Sunday best.

"Ernie!" Peter called hoarsely, "Get Pa."

The young boy turned and ran back through the iron gate and up the stone drive to the house. LooAnne assumed that this was one of the boys that Mrs. Andrews has spoken of when she first arrived; one of her two younger sons.

Within seconds of the boy disappearing the door was thrown open and Mr. Andrews emerged, followed by his wife, their two sons, and Clara all of whom were dressed for church.

Mr. Andrews ran to his son, relieving LooAnne of the slight burden on her shoulders. "What happened?" he asked, concern sounding in his voice.

"Oh Peter, are you alright?" exclaimed his mother as she took his beaten face in her hands and examined it.

"I'm fine, Ma," the young deputy assured before addressing his father. "Pa, there's a fella behind that house. He tried to kidnap Miss Nash -"

"Kidnap Miss Nash!" Mrs. Andrews cried, only then seeming to notice LooAnne's disheveled appearance.

Peter nodded. "Ya gotta get to him before he comes to and gets away," he told his father anxiously.

Mr. Andrews nodded and turned to his younger sons. "Ernest, help your brother back inside. Tony come with me."

The younger of the two boys wrapped Peter's arm around his shoulder and helped him through the gate with Mrs. Andrews close behind them. Clara laid her hand gently on LooAnne's arm and asked, "Are you alright, Miss Nash?" LooAnne smiled at the kind girl and nodded, "I'm perfectly alright, Clara. Your brother saved my life." Clara grinned broadly, obviously proud of her elder sibling. She and LooAnne followed Mrs. Andrews and her sons into the house, all the while wondering if Mr. Andrews and Tony would reach the kidnapper in time.

FIVE

Eavesdropper

"**A**lright, young man, that should hold you until it heals properly," the doctor said as he finished stitching the last of Peter's cuts.

The young deputy was sitting on a stool in the kitchen, his face creased with pain which he was trying his best to withstand. The doctor had stitched both cuts on his forehead and one on his cheek before telling him to get as much rest as he could throughout the weekend. The doctor had also given LooAnne an examination though she assured everyone that she was fine, just a bit shaken.

Mr. Andrews had found the attempted kidnapper still unconscious and, with the help of his son Tony, had taken him to jail but neither of them had yet returned.

"Peter you go directly to bed and I'll bring you some food," Mrs. Andrews commanded while the doctor packed his instruments into his bag.

"Ma, I'm fine," Peter argued as he tried to stand only to fall back on the stool as the room began to fade.

"Peter Matthew Andrews do not argue with me," his mother scolded.

"Your mother's right son," the doctor agreed as he started for the door. "You need to get all the rest you can, there's no tellin' what kinda head injury ya might have. Rest in a dark place for a few hours is best."

Peter sighed and nodded in defeat, allowing Ernest to help him to his parents' bedroom.

Mrs. Andrews turned to LooAnne and asked, "Are you sure you're alright, Miss Nash? Can I get you anything?"

LooAnne smiled and shook her head, "I'm perfectly alright, Mrs. Andrews. There's no need to worry over me. I'm only sorry I've caused so much trouble."

"Oh, Miss Nash, it was most certainly not your fault, dear. There was nothing you could have done to prevent it. I'm just glad you're not hurt."

"Thanks to your son, Mrs. Andrews. I'm quite indebted to him for saving me."

"I know he was glad to do it. He's wanted to be a police officer since he was a little boy."

"Well he makes a very good one. I'm sorry you missed services this morning on my account."

"Don't be sorry, Miss Nash. As I said it was not your fault. Did Miss Cathy and her brother ever show up?"

LooAnne frowned and shook her head, "No they didn't. I hope they're alright."

"I'm sure they are. If you want, I can send Ernest to check up on them. He goes to school with their younger sister so he knows where their house is."

"If he doesn't care to, that would be wonderful of him."

"Of course he doesn't. You go get cleaned up and I'll fetch Ernest."

"Thank you, Mrs. Andrews, I really do appreciate it."

LooAnne turned and made her way out of the kitchen to

the front hall, passing a few of the maids on her way. She slowly climbed the stairs to her room, feeling a wave of fatigue washing over her as the rush of adrenaline wore off. She shut the door to her room and immediately noticed her reflection in the mirror atop the bureau. Her hat was gone and her hair in disarray, her beautiful Sunday dress was rumpled and torn on the sleeve from where she had fallen. LooAnne sighed and dropped down on the bed, laying back to look up at the blue toile ceiling, but she seemed to see past this intricate design, searching deep within her for the answer to a question foremost in her mind. Who was that man? And how did she know him? She knew the answer was hidden deep within her and yet she could not seem to find it. His face was so familiar and his voice even more so. LooAnne closed her eyes and tried to imagine his face somewhere in her past. She searched her mind, going over the past few years, trying to remember how she knew this man, but with every memory she drew nothing but blanks. LooAnne sighed and rolled over on her bed, looking out the window at the far end of the room. Her mind was in a quandary as to how she knew this man. Just as she was about to close her eyes again she heard a soft knock on the door. LooAnne sat up and called, "Come in."

A moment later Clara entered with a glass of water in her hand. She smiled kindly at LooAnne who accepted the beverage with thanks.

"My father's downstairs. He said that they locked up the man and left one of the other deputies with him and that you need to come down to the sheriff's office some time tomorrow and press charges."

LooAnne nodded, "Alright, Clara. Thank you, and tell

your father thank you as well."

Clara smiled. "I will. Can I get you anything else, Miss Nash?"

LooAnne shook her head, "No, I think I'm going to get a little rest. Would you come up in about an hour and wake me?"

Clara nodded, "Of course, ma-am."

She turned and left the room, leaving LooAnne with her thoughts that tangled themselves about in her mind. She hoped that a short nap would clear her brain but found herself unable to sleep after only a few minutes of laying down. She decided to change out of her Sunday dress, hoping more comfortable attire would induce her sleep hormones.

She put on her light green jersey knit suit and removed her shoes and gloves, tossing them aside. She then sat down in one of the embroidered arm chairs, staring into the dark fireplace waiting for sleep to come. And soon it did...

LooAnne was awoken by a gentle hand shaking her shoulder. She stirred and then opened her eyes to find Clara standing beside her, smiling kindly as she always did. "I'm afraid I let you sleep in, Miss Nash," the young maid apologized.

LooAnne stretched a bit and yawned, feeling extremely refreshed. "What time is it?" she asked.

"It's after lunch, ma-am. I'm sorry but my mother said to let you sleep longer after what happened."

LooAnne shook her head and smiled, "It's alright, Clara. Your mother was quite right. I feel much better."

Clara returned LooAnne's smile and asked, "Do you want me to bring you something to eat, Miss Nash?"

"No thank you, I'm going to freshen up a bit and come downstairs to phone my uncle."

Clara nodded, "I'll get the cook to heat your lunch, ma-am. It'll be in the dining room."

LooAnne smiled at the kindly girl as she stood from the chair, "Thank you, Clara. I'll be down in a minute."

Clara left and LooAnne went to the bureau in search of her hair brush. After running it through her red hair and straightening her outfit LooAnne went downstairs to the phone in the entry hall. Telephones were scarce, especially out west, but with the Nash's great wealth came many luxuries. And this was one LooAnne found herself very appreciative of now that she could no longer talk to her uncle face to face.

She knew that he would need to know about what had happened that morning though she was sure he would be very upset by the fact that his niece had almost been kidnapped.

LooAnne picked up the telephone and asked the operator for the Nash Estate. Not long after she heard the very familiar voice of her uncle's steward, Chris Block, one of Ricky's most trusted friends.

"Hello?"

"Mr. Block, it's LooAnne, may I speak with Uncle Ricky please?"

"Why of course, Miss Nash," the middle-aged man agreed readily. "I'm sure he'll be very glad to hear from you."

However much LooAnne loved talking to her uncle, she was certain that on this particular day he would not like what she had to say.

"Thank you, Mr. Block," she said, trying to keep her nerves from sounding in her voice.

"No problem, Miss Nash. It'll be just a minute."

After a few moments of silence LooAnne heard the one voice that eased all the anxiety within her.

"LooAnne?" her uncle's kind, strong voice met her ears making her realize how much she missed him.

"Yes Uncle Ricky, it's me."

"It's very good to hear your voice, my dear." LooAnne could almost see the smile on her uncle's face as he spoke.

"It's good to hear yours too, Uncle Ricky. I – um – I'm afraid we've had a bit of trouble here that I think you should know about."

"Trouble?" her uncle questioned. "What kind of trouble?"

"Well you see, I was on my way to church this morning -" LooAnne paused, knowing that what she had to say would be very disconcerting to her uncle, "and there was a man standing on the street and – well – he tried to kidnap me."

"Kidnap you!" her uncle yelled so loudly that LooAnne had to pull the phone away from her ear.

"What happened? Are you alright?" his voice no longer held its usual kind tone, but one of mixed fear and anger.

"I'm perfectly fine. Mrs. Andrews' son, who happens to be a deputy, came along just in time. He saved my life."

LooAnne heard her uncle sigh in relief and could imagine him running his hand through his graying black hair.

"Thank goodness for that," he spoke with obvious strain in his voice. "Do you have any idea who it was?"

"I've been racking my brain to find out that very thing. I'm sure I know him from somewhere but so help me I can't remember."

"You're sure you've seen him before?" her uncle questioned.

"I'm absolutely sure. He was at the train station when I

arrived and I-"

"He was at the train station?" her uncle exclaimed.

"Yes," LooAnne admitted. "He was watching me just as he was today before he tried to take me. Once he caught me I tried to fight him off but couldn't which is strange because it was as if he expected every move I tried to pull on him." There was silence on the line and LooAnne was beginning to wonder if they had been disconnected when her uncle's strained voice spoke, "LooAnne, are you certain it wasn't a Luther?"

This thought struck LooAnne with renewed fear. It had not occurred to her that the man who had tried to abduct her could be a member of her father's family simply because she thought they had long since been run out of the area, but now that the thought was in her mind it all seemed to make sense. The reason he had known how to stop her strategies to escape, the reason he looked so familiar to her, his entire purpose in taking her to begin with would all make sense if he was indeed a Luther!

"LooAnne, are you alright?" he uncle's voice broke into LooAnne's disturbed thoughts.

"Y-yes, I'm alright. I just – do you really think he was a member of my family?"

"You would know better than me, my dear," Ricky said. "But you say he knew how to stop you from getting away, and that he looked familiar to you. Do you think it could have been?"

LooAnne went over the all too familiar faces of the cruel family whom she had lived with from birth until age twelve. But it had been almost seven years since she had last seen them face to face and she knew that many of them must have changed quite significantly.

"It could have been any one of my cousins that are still alive or out of prison," LooAnne mused aloud. "He seemed a bit older than me and most of them were." LooAnne heard her uncle sigh on the other end. "Let's not get ahead of ourselves. Maybe it wasn't a Luther at all?" LooAnne shook her head, "But I'm beginning to think that it was, Uncle Ricky. That's the only way it really makes sense."

"But why would the Luther want you...unless..." Ricky didn't finish as reality hit the both of them.

"They know who I am," LooAnne whispered, looking around her to make certain no one was listening. "That's the only reason they would want to take me!"

"LooAnne, don't get ahead of yourself, you don't know that."

"But why else would the Luther's want me?"

"Did he act like he knew you?" Ricky asked.

"Not really, not as Beth Luther anyway. He called me Miss Nash."

"Well at least that leaves room for reasonable doubt. Had he known your true identity he would have most certainly made you aware of it immediately."

LooAnne nodded though her uncle could not see her. "I only hope your right. But what other explanation is there?"

"Have you spoken with the sheriff at all since it happened?" her uncle asked.

"No not yet. He wants me to come sometime in the morning and press charges against the man."

"He'll more than likely ask you if you can identify him. Even if you can don't let on to the sheriff that you know him. The man will be jailed whether you know him or not so there's no reason to tell the sheriff anything besides what happened yesterday."

"But, Uncle Ricky, if it is a Luther and he knows who I am, what's to stop him from telling the sheriff himself?" LooAnne failed in attempt to hide the desperation in her voice and heard her uncle sigh heavily.

"LooAnne, we can't hide you forever. If it happens as you think it could, I want you to come home where you'll be protected."

"But Uncle Ricky you'll be ruined!" LooAnne exclaimed. "Your reputation, the Nash family, everything! No one will do business with you when they find out you've been hiding a Luther for almost seven years!"

It was at this moment that LooAnne's rattled nerves were snapped by the sudden intake of breath behind her! She whirled around, letting a gasp of her own escape her lips! Her eyes widened with fear as she clutched the phone tightly in her hand and stared into the shocked face of Peter Andrews!

SIX

Missing...Murder.

The air in the entry hall was thick with tension as LooAnne stood frozen under the awed stare of the young deputy. He stood before her, his eyes wide with shock at what he had just heard.

LooAnne met his stare, fear washing over her as her heart began to thud against her chest. Only the very faint voice of her uncle from the telephone caused her to slowly lift the earpiece. "I've got to go, Uncle Ricky," she said, not taking her eyes from Peter Andrews' beaten face.

"Alright," Ricky agreed realizing she was no longer at liberty to talk. "You call me tomorrow when you get back from the sheriff's office, and if anything happens come straight home!"

LooAnne nodded, "I will, Uncle Ricky. Goodbye."

"Goodbye, LooAnne."

LooAnne hung the earpiece back on the telephone, ending the call but not once allowing her gaze to waver. She stared into Peter Andrews' eyes, her mind and heart both racing with fear and uncertainty and a feeling she could not seem to distinguish. What was he going to do? Would he tell his family what he had heard? Would he be repulsed by her? Would he be the one to reveal her haunting secret to the world?

LooAnne decided she had to do something to break the pressing silence. "Please," she whispered, her voice steady although she begged, "don't say anything. You don't have to have anything to do with me or my family, but please don't tell anyone?"

The young deputy stared at her for a moment, seeming undecided as to what he should say. But then his shocked expression slowly melted away, his face softening. Peter shook his head, "I won't say anything."

LooAnne felt herself release a breath she didn't know she had been holding as the weight was lifted from her shoulders but she suddenly felt very uncomfortable under his stare.

"Thank you, Deputy," she whispered before turning and walking briskly up the stairs. The feeling of his eyes on her as she ascended caused tingles to run down her spine. LooAnne went straight to her room, shutting the door forcefully behind her. She could still feel her heart beating against her chest as she stood in the midst of the bedroom, staring at the far wall blankly. How could she have spoken so carelessly of such a precious secret? Why had she not been more guarded when she knew fully well that the possibility of someone overhearing was so great? LooAnne's mind reprimanded her again and again for her stupidity. She had only met Peter Andrews a mere two hours before and had no reason to trust that he would keep his word. But now there was nothing to be done. She had no choice but to believe the young deputy when he promised not to tell her true identity to the world.

LooAnne sank down in one of the embroidered chairs and closed her eyes, trying to ease the anxiety she felt, but it was of no use.

"I'm such a fool," she whispered to herself.

"Are you alright, Miss Nash?" LooAnne was so startled by the sudden feminine voice that she nearly fell from her seat! Her eyes shot open but she sighed with relief upon seeing that it was only Clara standing in the open doorway.

"I'm sorry, ma-am," Clara apologized timidly. "I didn't mean to startle you but no one answered when I knocked."

"It-it's alright, Clara," LooAnne assured, placing a hand on her thumping heart. "I didn't hear you knock, is there something you wanted?"

"Ernest got back from the Morrison's and said that no one was home. Mama sent him to church to see if Miss Cathy and her brother were there but he said they weren't. He doesn't know where they are, Miss Nash."

LooAnne instantly became concerned over her missing friends. She had not known Cathy long but knew her well enough to know that she was not one to forgo a premade engagement. And now that it was confirmed she and her brother could not be found elsewhere, LooAnne was beginning to wonder if they had been the victims of foul play!

"Does your mother know where they might be?" she asked, rising from her chair.

Clara shook her head, "No, ma-am. She's mighty worried herself. It's not like any of the Morrison's to miss services."

"Do they have any relations nearby they could be with?"

Again Clara shook her head, "Their parents were killed a few years ago during a bank robbery. They don't have any

63

other family out west."

LooAnne sighed and looked down into the fire as her mind raced. She was in a quandary as to why the brother and sister had seemed to disappear. No answer she came up with seemed logical until she thought of the man who had tried to abduct her. Did he have anything to do with their failure to appear that morning and their apparent disappearance now?

LooAnne looked back up at Clara and said, "Is anyone out looking for them?"

"Yes, Cathy's beau Dave James, came back with Ernest and said that he was looking for them too. He and Peter have gone to search the area."

LooAnne nodded and sighed, "I suppose there's nothing we can do but wait." She sat back down on the edge of her chair, resting her elbows on her knees as she looked into the dark fireplace. "I hope they're alright."

"I'm sure they are, ma-am," Clara tried to boost LooAnne's spirits. "Maybe one of them got sick overnight and they had to go to the doctor this morning or something like that?"

LooAnne smiled grimly at Clara's attempt to help the situation. "I hope you're right, Clara." Her smile broadened a bit as she asked, "I didn't know Cathy had a suitor?"

Clara grinned and nodded, "Dave and Peter have been good friends since school. They're both deputies now and Dave has always had his eye on Cathy."

"Well I hope he treats her well," LooAnne said honestly, thinking of how she had been treated by her first love.

"Oh I know he will," Clara assured. "I've met him many times and he's a perfect gentleman."

LooAnne smiled, "Good. I look forward to meeting him."
It was this statement that cause a shadow to fall over
Clara's face as she looked down at the carpeted floor.
LooAnne cocked her head a bit and asked, "Is something
wrong?"

"No, ma-am, I'm just worried about Stephen," Clara
admitted. "He was supposed to meet me at the gate early
this morning before anyone woke up. Not to run away, but
to talk about it. I was there but he never showed up and I
haven't heard from him. That's so unlike him, Miss Nash."
Clara looked up at LooAnne exposing the worry in her
eyes. "I'm afraid those men who were after him might
have hurt him."

LooAnne's frown deepened. "I don't know what to tell
you, Clara," she admitted. "Are you certain you got the
time and day right?"

Clara nodded vigorously. "Very certain, ma-am. Oh, Miss
Nash, I'm so afraid he's been hurt by those men and I don't
know what to do to help him!"

LooAnne stood up and laid a comforting hand on Clara's
shoulder. "Maybe he was just unavoidably detained? He
might come and see you later on today and explain his
absence."

Clara nodded, "I hope your right, Miss Nash. I feel so
helpless; there's no one I can go to if he doesn't come
back."

"He will," LooAnne tried to sound more confident than
she felt. For all either of them knew he could have run off
for good with no intention of returning, but she couldn't
tell that to Clara.

"I'm so sorry to burden you with all this, Miss Nash,"
Clara added, looking as guilty as she felt. "You're the only

one that knows about Stephen so I can't tell anyone else."

"But, Clara, you could," LooAnne objected. "You could tell your mother and father, I'm sure they would understand."

"Oh no, Miss Nash!" Clara exclaimed. "I could never betray Stephan's trust. He's in trouble somehow and us seeing each other is risky as it is. I can't imagine what might happen if my family knew. They might tell him not to come back!"

"They would just be protecting you, Clara," LooAnne said gently. "Your parents only want what's best for you."

"I know they do, but Stephen told me not to tell anyone about him and I can't go back on my word."

"You told me," LooAnne pointed out.

"I know but you found out. I had to."

LooAnne sighed and nodded, "Clara, it's none of my business whether or not you tell your parents. That's your decision, but I do want you to be very careful of this man. I don't mean to imply that he would hurt you, but you don't know about the so called men who are apparently after him. By coming here Stephen is putting you in danger you know?"

Clara looked down and nodded, "I know, and he knows it too. We're always very careful and he almost never comes here."

LooAnne smiled reassuringly and said, "Why don't you go ask the cook to whip up something for an early supper and we can both wait for Peter to get back with news on Cathy and Bill?"

Clara returned LooAnne's smile and nodded. "Alright, thank you so much, Miss Nash."

"You're very welcome."

Clara turned and walked out the door and down the hall, leaving LooAnne lost in thoughts of their conversation. She was inclined to think that Stephen Parker had left of his own accord with no intention of marrying Clara. Either he had realized the danger he was causing her or he had seen her as too much of a crutch to carry on their engagement. However, both scenarios were very likely and there was still the chance that Clara had been right, and the men who were chasing him had caught up to their foe.

No matter what had happened LooAnne doubted that they would ever see the ambiguous Stephen Parker again. She could only hope that the same was not to be said about Bill and Cathy Morrison.

LooAnne straightened the wrinkles from her skirt and then headed downstairs to the dining room where one of the maids was setting the table.

"Good evening, ma-am," she curtsied slightly.

"Good evening," LooAnne smiled as she took her seat. The maid left to fetch the small meal LooAnne had requested and returned a moment later. LooAnne ate in silence and found the atmosphere very lonely after being used to eating with either her uncle or his ward present. She could not help the feeling of homesickness that overcame her, and the want to return to the only member of her family who had ever loved her.

She had almost finished eating when the sound of the iron door opening in the entry hall disturbed the silence in the house and an animated voice followed it!

"Mom! Pa! Get down here!" LooAnne instantly recognized the voice as belonging to Peter Andrews. She arose from her seat so quickly that it almost toppled over backwards, and ran into the entry hall just as Mr. and Mrs.

Andrews and Clara came running from various directions. The moment LooAnne laid eyes on the situation her heart sank! There was Cathy, being supported by the arms of who LooAnne assumed was Dave James! Her eyes were red with tears that looked as though they had been staining her face for hours. In Peter's arms was the limp body of a young girl no more than eight or nine, she looked as though she had cried herself into exhaustion and now was sleeping peacefully against the young deputy's shoulder

"Oh, Peter, what happened?" Mrs. Andrews cried as she ran to assist her son.

"LooAnne!" Cathy exclaimed when she caught sight of her friend. She broke away from the blond-headed young man and threw her arms around LooAnne's neck. "Oh, LooAnne, they killed him!" she sobbed. "He's dead!"

"What? Who?" LooAnne gasped, feeling her heart rate rise within her.

"Bill!" Cathy chocked out.

LooAnne felt her stomach begin to tighten as she hugged Cathy closer. "What?" she whispered, unable to make her voice more audible.

"We found them at the downtown hospital," came Peter's grim baritone. "The doc said Bill had just passed away from a bullet wound."

"A bullet wound!" Mrs. Andrews exclaimed.

Peter nodded. "I told Cathy she and her sister could stay here for the night. I hope that's alright, Miss Nash?"

LooAnne was surprised that Peter had addressed her at all considering what he had heard earlier that morning, but she answered readily. "Of course, they can stay as long as they like. Mrs. Andrews let's get them to the room next to mine."

The housekeeper nodded vigorously and assisted LooAnne in helping Cathy up the stairs with Clara, Peter, and Dave following close behind.

Mrs. Andrews opened the door to a bedroom right next to LooAnne's. She directed Peter to lay the young girl on the bed while LooAnne helped Cathy take a seat on the chaise lounge.

The lamenting girl buried her face in her hands, her shoulders shaking with sobs. LooAnne sat down at her side and placed a gentle arm around her crumpled frame. "Cathy," she whispered softly, trying to ease her friend's cries, "please, is there anything we can do?"

Cathy only shook her head, unable to speak as she choked on the overgrown knot in her aching throat.

Dave James stood over Cathy and LooAnne, his face creased with pain and helplessness as he watched her cry. His brown felt Stetson, bearing the same star as Peter's, was clenched tightly in one hand while the other ran repeatedly through his dirty-blond hair. LooAnne looked up at the young man who was obviously at a loss to know what to do. Moisture gathered behind his light brown eyes as he stared helplessly at Cathy sobbing in LooAnne's arms.

After a moment of uncertainty, the deputy knelt before his love and placed a careful hand on her shoulder.

"Cathy, please," he whispered, his voice higher and a bit more boyish than Peter's, confirming LooAnne's thoughts that he was a few years younger. "I'll find him, Cathy, I'll find the man who did this, I swear I will!" he vowed.

Cathy lifted her head from her hands and stared into Dave's loving eyes. She was still gasping, trying to get control of her labored breathing, but she nodded, looking at Dave as though he were the only person in the room. "Thank you," she choked out, her voice hoarse and pained. Dave smiled reassuringly and planting a gentle kiss on Cathy's forehead before taking her into his arms. LooAnne stood to allow Dave the opportunity to calm Cathy as she was sure only he could. Mrs. Andrews was in the midst of covering Cathy's slumbering sister with an afghan and Clara was standing in the doorway watching tearfully. LooAnne went to her side and asked, "Did your brother say what exactly happened?"

Clara shook her head, "No, he brought Karen up here and then went downstairs to talk to Pa. Who would do such a thing, Miss Nash?" she asked, drying a tear from the corner of her eye.

LooAnne shook her head, "I don't know, Clara. Someone void of all feeling and human dignity."

LooAnne then turned and left the room without another word. She had to know what had happened that resulted in Bill Morrison's death and she knew the only way to find that out would be to talk with Peter Andrews, one of the only men on earth who knew her true identity.

LooAnne made her way down the hall and ivory staircase to the entry hall which was vacant except for the low hum of men's voices coming from around the corner.

LooAnne's walk was slow, the thought of having to speak with the young deputy causing her nerves to tingle. She could only imagine what he thought of her, the offspring of a family known throughout Texas as murderers and thieves, hiding under the name of one of the most astute businessman in the country. She hated the thought of Peter Andrews disliking her though she did not quite know why; perhaps because he had saved her life and she wanted somehow to repay him, to be given the chance to prove she was not like her father's cruel family. She wanted his good favor but she knew that had been lost with the unintended revelation of her deepest secret.

LooAnne rounded the corner and saw Peter and his father talking just beneath the stairs, both looking grim.

LooAnne took a deep breath and approached them. They were both so engrossed in their conversation that they did not see her until she was nearly upon them.

Mr. Andrews looked up questioningly, drawing his son's attention. "Can I help you, Miss Nash?" he asked.

Peter turned around and looked somewhat surprised to see LooAnne directly behind him.

"I'm sorry for interrupting you, Mr. Andrews. I was hoping one of you could tell me what exactly happened? Why was Bill killed?"

"I wish I knew that myself," Peter spoke, his voice low and calm. "Dave and I decided to check the hospital first thing. They had been there for about an hour. Doc said Bill had been brought in with a bullet wound in the stomach, he said he did everything he could but it wasn't enough." Peter sighed and shook his head, "I ain't sure what exactly happened. All Doc knew was that some fella had seen Bill get shot when the Morrison's left their house this morning and helped Cathy and Karen to the hospital. Bill never had come to after the shooting, he died when the doc tried to perform surgery. Dave and I got there only about twenty minutes after it happened. Cathy and Karen were too hysterical to tell us anything and Doc said they were in shock and needed rest so he gave them something to make them sleep once we brought 'em over here. Karen was so exhausted she fell asleep before we could even give her the medication."

LooAnne nodded, her heart aching for Cathy and her sister. "Who would want to kill Bill?" she asked mournfully.

Peter shook his head, "I don't know. He was a good friend o' mine, one of the kindest men I've ever known. I can't imagine who would do such an awful thing."

Despite his calm tone of voice, it was obvious that Peter was shaken by Bill's death. Anger and sadness shown in his eyes as he spoke of his friend's fatal attack.

"Have you spoken to the sheriff yet?" Mr. Andrews asked his son.

Peter shook his head, "No, he was busy with the man who brought Bill in. I'm gonna head over there as soon as Dave comes down and see what he found out."

Mr. Andrews nodded and said, "I've got to get back to work, let me know when you hear anything, Pete. Excuse me Miss Nash," the butler bowed slightly before turning to disappear towards the house office, leaving LooAnne and Peter alone.

An awkward silence befell the two and LooAnne felt her nerves swelling within her as a growing pit formed in her stomach. Fearing that Peter would bring up the incident from earlier that day she turned and was about to walk away when she was stopped by his somber voice uttering her name quietly and yet in such a way that her body felt compelled to stop and hear him.

"Miss Nash."

LooAnne froze in her tracks, her heart beating wildly, willing the tenseness of the situation to pass. For a moment all was quiet, she stared at the big iron door, waiting for the deputy to speak, fearing what he would say.

"I know that – that what I heard was a very precious secret," he addressed her back, his deep baritone speaking quietly so no one else would hear. "I just wanted to reassure you that I won't tell anyone and that I don't hold it against you."

LooAnne felt a knot growing in her throat as she heard his last words. She had never imagined anyone not holding such a terrible thing against her, not to judge her for the family she had been born into; but now it appeared that Peter Andrews was not and it bewildered her. How could he not hate her for being the progeny of an evil clan who had taken so many lives? Who had been trained to kill and taught that no life was worth more than the Luther's own desire to have whatever they wanted.

For a moment she stood in silence, staring into nothing as her mind molded its self around the words he had just uttered. Then she turned, ready to face him.

He was no longer there...

SEVEN

Recognition

LooAnne didn't see Peter again until the next morning when she was scheduled to go to the Sheriff's Office to press charges against the man who tried to kidnap her. Cathy and her sister, Karen, had both benefited from the drug the doctor had given them to sleep and they slept most of the day and through the night. Dave didn't leave Cathy's side until she was asleep and then he and Peter left to find out from the sheriff what exactly had happened. Peter had not returned as he had the night shift meaning the occupants of Belle Hall had to wait until the following day to hear the story in full.

Peter was to return at noon and accompany LooAnne and Cathy to the sheriff's office where Cathy would tell Sheriff Elliot her account of the killing and LooAnne would venture to identify the man who had attacked her; a man who could, if he was the man she feared him to be, turn the tables and identify her as the daughter of Jason Luther. LooAnne tried her best to distract her mind from such an event as she readied herself to leave. She stared blankly into the mirror as Clara finished putting small finger waves into her bobbed red hair. She imagined herself standing face to face with one of her relations, being humiliated for who she was. Him telling the world that she was the daughter of one of the most feared Luther's; a girl who had been forced to help her vile family steal and kill. If that man who attacked her were in fact a Luther, he could turn her entire life upside down and ruin her and her uncle forever.

"Miss Nash, are you alright?" Clara's kind voice broke into LooAnne's thoughts.

She looked up at her maid's worried expression and smiled, "Yes Clara, I'm fine."

"You look upset, ma-am," Clara persisted.

LooAnne stood from the vanity and shook her head, "Not upset, just nervous."

"There's no reason to be worried, ma-am," Clara assured her, "he can't do anything from behind bars."

LooAnne smiled and nodded, "You're right of course, but I can't help but be a little worried." All the while thinking, *if only that were true.*

Clara said no more on the topic and accompanied LooAnne to the room Cathy and her sister were occupying. Karen had not said a word since her brother's death which weighed heavily on Cathy's mind. She tried every way she knew to get her sister to speak, but the distressed child remained dolefully silent. She ate little and had not once left their room. Her sister's condition added greatly to Cathy's sadness but the more she tried to boost Karen's spirits the deeper into depression the girl sank. LooAnne knocked on their door and heard Cathy's strained voice call for her and Clara to enter. Karen was laying on the bed looking out the window at two small sparrows that had landed on the sill, Cathy was seated at her sister's side already dressed for their outing.

"I hate to leave her, LooAnne," Cathy's voice was hoarse from hours of crying and she had dark bags beneath her reddened eyes.

"Maybe she'd like to come with us? Some time out of this room might do her good," LooAnne suggested.

Cathy turned to Karen and laid a tender hand on her arm, "Honey, do you wanna come with me and LooAnne?"

Karen only shook her head, not once taking her eyes from the window sill.

Cathy's frown deepened though she had expected such an answer. "Please, Karen? We can stop at the grocery and get some of those chocolates you like?"

Again Karen shook her head, not the slightest bit tempted by her sister's offer.

Cathy was about to say something when there was a knock at the door.

"Come in," LooAnne called.

The door was opened, revealing Dave James and Peter Andrews standing in the hall, their hats in hand. Dave cast a forlorn smile at the ladies and asked, "Y'all ready?"

Cathy looked down at the sheets and shook her head, "I can't just leave her here like this, Dave."

The young deputy frowned and entered the room. He took a seat beside Cathy on the bed and leaned over Karen's limp body. "What's wrong, Butterfly?" he asked, calling the child by her pet name.

Karen's eyes began to swell with tears as she turned her head away from the window, at last, to look at Dave. "That man," she whispered, her voice so thick and quiet that it was almost not heard.

Dave frowned, "What man, Darlin'?"

"The man who – who killed B-Bill," Karen choked out.

"What about him?"

"He-he said he would take me."

Everyone in the room was shocked upon hearing this and Dave withdrew slightly, confused and surprised by Karen's statement.

"Honey, what are you talking about?" Cathy asked.

"The man – came to s-see Bill. He said he w-would k-k-kill Bill and t-take me a-away if Bill didn't t-tell him."

"Tell him what, Butterfly?" Dave asked.

"Where Ben is," Karen said before she burst into a fit of tears.

Dave picked her up in his arms and rocked her gently, trying to calm her down. "It's alright, Karen, you don't have to be scared, he won't take you, I promise."

Karen continued to cry and Cathy's eyes were becoming watery as well. LooAnne's mind, however, was racing with all the new facts about the killing and the memories of past relations. Though she knew it had nothing to do with the present, Ben had been the name of one of her brothers and hearing it said caused a small pang within her.

Putting all this aside LooAnne focused on the task at hand, knowing that Karen had just added a great deal of information to her brother's killing.

When she had first started speaking of 'the man' LooAnne had thought she had had a dream, but now she knew that the poor child had obviously seen or heard something that led to the death of Bill Morrison. If they could only find out who Ben was, then maybe they could find the killer! Apparently Dave had thought the same thing because he asked gently, "Butterfly, do you know who Ben is?"

Karen shook her head, keeping her face buried deep in Dave's chest.

"When did your brother tell the man about Ben?" he persisted, not wanting to upset the child further but desperate to catch the murderer.

"The-the other day. He-he said he knew Bill could t-tell him wh-where Ben was but Bill w-wouldn't."

"That must be why he was killed," Peter spoke for the first time. All eyes turned on him and he said, "Bill knew where this Ben fella was and wouldn't tell, so the worthless scum who was lookin' for him carried out his threat and killed him."

"Cathy, do you know anyone named Ben?" Dave asked. She shook her head, looking very perplexed. "I've never heard of anyone by that name before," she said. "As far as I know Bill hadn't either."

"But he obviously had," Peter spoke again.

"I don't understand," Cathy whispered, her eyes starting to tear.

Dave laid a comforting hand on her shoulder. "I don't either, but we will, and once we do we'll have the man who killed him." He then turned to Karen who's crying had calmed a bit. "You wanna come with us, Butterfly?" She shook her head and sniffled.

"I can stay with her, Miss Morrison," Clara offered. "I won't leave her side 'til y'all get back."

Cathy thought a moment then nodded, "Thank you, Clara. We'll be back as soon as we can."

Clara smiled and took Karen from Dave's arms. The young deputy planted a kiss on the girl's forehead and then followed the rest of the party downstairs where the chauffeur was waiting with the sedan on the stone drive,

Peter's automobile not far behind it.

LooAnne and Cathy got in the sedan and their chauffeur started for the Sheriff's Office which was only a few blocks away, Peter and Dave not far behind. LooAnne's eyes studied her passing surroundings carefully as they drove, trying to get to know the city better since she was to spend the majority of the next few years there.

She noticed right away how many people there were in the city; bustling about on their daily errands or to and from work. LooAnne found herself becoming somewhat homesick at the sight of all the strangers and unfamiliar places. In Decatur she had known nearly every occupant of the small town and was free to roam its streets without the fear of losing her way; and most importantly, she had been able to go home to a place of safety where she was among loved ones.

But now, stuck in Dallas where the need to be educated for her future business dealings, overruled her inward desire to never leave the safe haven she had in the Nash Estate. She felt very misplaced and unsafe among people who didn't know of her past and could not protect her from it as her uncle could. The only person in the city of Dallas, one of the only men in the entire world, who knew of her secret followed directly behind her, and she had yet to find out if she could trust him enough to keep his promise as he had declared. LooAnne could only hope that he was the honest, upright man he appeared to be.

Only a few minutes after their departure the foursome arrived in downtown Dallas which was crowded with people, vehicles, and vendors. Lights were flashing everywhere and the noise was very great. Venues and theaters lined the streets with the very popular Ritz and

Perk Palace among them. LooAnne was in awe, having never seen such a large city so full and bustling. The chauffeur drove down Elm Street and then turned to the left where he went a few blocks before stopping in front of a large brick building that read: *"Dallas County Sheriff's Department"*

LooAnne felt her heart speed up and her nerves tighten as she was faced with the building that might hold one of her long lost relatives, a man who might recognize her as Beth Luther and tell the world, if for no other reason than to ruin her life and the life of her uncle forever.

Peter and Dave got out and opened the rear doors for the ladies. Dave smiled kindly and took Cathy's hand, leading her up the steps to the door. LooAnne alighted and looked up at the two story building, reluctant to go inside.

"Miss Nash?" Peter's voice jarred LooAnne from her thoughts and she realized her companions were already at the door of the building.

"Oh, I'm sorry," LooAnne apologized as she joined them.

"Are you alright, LooAnne?" Cathy asked.

LooAnne nodded and ventured a smile, "Perfectly fine. Just awed by the big city."

The trio nodded, accepting this answer, and they all continued inside.

The interior was much like any office LooAnne had ever seen. There was a desk in the front where a young woman sat typing away on a typewriter, her thin hands moving quickly over the keys. The walls were papered in a dull gold print with pictures of former officials lining them and there was a waiting area of five armchairs to the left. Directly behind the desk was a door which read: *"Sheriff Tom Elliot"*

The young secretary at the desk looked up from her typing and smiled a shy smile. Her blond hair framed her face perfectly and curled under her chin, she wore a pair of thin eyeglasses, somewhat magnifying her bright blue eyes.

"Good morning, Peter, Dave." she greeted. "Oh and Cathy I'm so sorry to hear about your brother."

Cathy nodded, "Thank you, Gladys."

"And who is this young lady?" the secretary asked, referring to LooAnne.

LooAnne smiled, "I'm LooAnne Nash."

"Oh it's very nice to meet you, Miss Nash," she smiled, her eye-brows raised as she looked at LooAnne in awe.

"A pleasure to meet you too," LooAnne returned, smiling kindly at the secretary.

"Tom's waiting for you in the office, Peter," she told the young deputy.

He nodded and led the way through the door behind the desk with LooAnne, Cathy, and Dave following.

The next room was an office looking much like the first only with less décor. There was a cedar desk pulled towards the front, piled with stacks of papers, pencils, and a small lamp with a rack of firearms displayed behind it. To the side was a small table with two chairs on either side and a coat rack stood by the door. The walls were bare except for a door leading to the back of the building, iron bars lining its single window.

Behind the desk sat a man much younger than LooAnne had expected. Muscular and clean shaven, he looked to be in his early thirties with a head full of short, black curls. He wore a sheriff's uniform matching Peter and Dave's and a tin star pinned proudly on his chest pocket. He stood up when the foursome entered and nodded at the ladies,

"Howdy, Cathy. And I'm assumin' you're Miss LooAnne Nash?"

LooAnne nodded, "Yes sir, Sheriff..."

"Elliot, Tom Elliot." The Sheriff came from behind his desk and said, "I'm sorry about what happened yesterday, Miss Nash. A poor way to welcome you to our city."

LooAnne shook her head, "It could have been much worse, Sheriff," she assured him.

Sheriff Elliot nodded, "I hear that if Peter hadn't heard you screamin' it would o' been."

The sheriff glanced at his deputy who frowned slightly and shook his head, "It was nothin'," he said simply.

Elliot snorted, "Tell that to your face, Pete."

Peter only shrugged, his quiet nature withholding his inward thoughts, thoughts that LooAnne found herself very intrigued by. She yearned to know what he was thinking when she could see that his thoughts were deep and sometimes unsettled as they had been when he spoke of his friend's death.

"Cathy, I'm very sorry about your brother," the sheriff went on. "I promise you we're doing all we can to find the scoundrel who did it. The witness said that y'all had just walked outta the house when it happened."

Cathy looked down and nodded, "We were leaving to pick up LooAnne for church. We just got out the door and there – there was a shot almost immediately," tears began to gather in Cathy's eyes as she went on. "Karen screamed and for a moment I didn't know what had happened until I saw Bill on the ground by the door..." Cathy couldn't finish as she broke down into another fit of tears at the memory of her brother's so sudden death.

Dave was at her side instantly, trying to console her.

Sheriff Elliot sighed and turned to LooAnne, "If you wouldn't mind coming to the back to take a look at that prisoner it might be just as well that we give these two a minute?"

LooAnne agreed, though her heart was beating wildly. She was finally going to come face to face with the man who had tried to abduct her the day before, a man she feared she would recognize!

Sheriff Elliot donned some keys from his desk and unlocked the door behind it revealing a hall of barred cells. LooAnne followed him down the hall with Peter behind them. They passed three prisoners sleeping heavily on straw cots whom LooAnne assumed were either drunks or sneak thieves, both of which were very common in the city. She didn't recognize any of them until they reached the cell which sat against the far corner.

Like the others, this man was laid out on his cot only he was not sleeping. His dark brown eyes stared at the ceiling impassively until he heard the threesome stop in front of his cell. He turned his head and almost instantly locked eyes with LooAnne, his face taking on an inscrutable glare.

LooAnne had tried her best to go over the faces of her cousins in her mind, to derive what they would look like now that they were older; but now, as she stared into the face of her attacker, she saw for the first time a vision of past days. Memories of her childhood flooded her and quenched her heart. She felt a knot beginning to grow in her throat as they stared at one another in silence, but she knew that she must not give anything away, she could not let them know...

"Do you recognize him at all, Miss Nash?" Sheriff Elliot

asked, the sudden presence of his voice startling LooAnne a bit.

"No," she answered quietly. "I've never seen him before yesterday."

"He doesn't look the least bit familiar to you?"

LooAnne shook her head, still staring into the darkened eyes that looked back at her with loathsome distaste.

"Not in the least bit," LooAnne said, hiding the tent of falsehood in her voice.

"But you're sure that was the man who tried to kidnap you?" Sheriff Elliot continued.

LooAnne nodded, longing to be out of the man's presence. "Very sure," she verified.

Sheriff Elliot nodded, "Well, you be sure he'll go away for a long time to come."

It was this statement that the criminal could not surpass without commenting factually. "I wouldn't be so sure, Sheriff," he snorted, lifting an eyebrow at his visitors. "I'm gonna get outta here, you can bet on it!"

"You're not in a position to make threats, mister," Sheriff Elliot informed the man, "You're goin' to prison for a long time for what you done and there ain't nothin' you can do about it."

"We'll see about that won't we?" the man smirked before turning his eyes on LooAnne, "I'll be seein' ya soon, Miss Nash. Watch yourself."

LooAnne felt a chill run down her spine as the man addressed her with such surety. She wanted to turn and run from the building, to get away from this man whose presence gave her such emotional unease that she could barely contain it. LooAnne wished more than anything that she could be in the safety of the Nash Estate where her uncle could protect her, but she took hold of her emotions and restrained them, knowing that she must not act so as to give away her secret to the sheriff and his deputy, one of who's intent stare she could feel against her back as the sheriff angrily scolded his prisoner.

LooAnne saw no reason to further torment herself and started walking briskly back down the hall, feeling the presence of Peter Andrews close behind her.

LooAnne opened the door to Sheriff Elliot's office and found Dave and Cathy talking quietly, her tears slowing as Dave reassured her. They both looked up when LooAnne and Peter walked through the door. Cathy sniffled a bit and asked, "Did you recognize him, LooAnne?"

LooAnne shook her head and looked down, her conscience not allowing her to lie to Cathy without a look of sorrow on her face. "No, I don't know who he is."

"But I thought you said you recognized him from somewhere before?"

"I thought I did," LooAnne said. "But now that I look closer I – I don't think I've ever seen him before."

Cathy nodded, accepting this explanation and before anyone could comment further Sheriff Elliot walked through the door. He closed and locked it with his set of keys and then turned apologetic eyes on LooAnne. "I'm sorry about him, Miss Nash. He's a wily one."

"It's alright, Sheriff, I'm just glad he's behind bars where he belongs."

"You can be sure he'll stay there, Miss Nash," Sheriff Elliot assured her, though to little effect.

LooAnne smiled and thanked all three lawmen for the time and effort they had put into helping both her and Cathy. "If you gentlemen would please excuse me I think I'll head back to Belle Hall, my classes start in a week and I've not even finished unpacking."

"And I need to check on Karen," Cathy added.

Sheriff Elliot nodded and said, "Cathy if you can think of anything else that might be helpful in catching Bill's killer let me or Dave know, alright?"

Cathy nodded, promising to do just that, and then Dave and Peter walked both girls back to the sedan where the chauffeur was waiting. He immediately alighted from the driver's seat and opened the back door for LooAnne and Cathy who climbed in. Both girls rode in silence, each of them affected by the emotional visit to the Sheriff's Office. LooAnne could only imagine how hard it was for Cathy to bear the loss of her older brother, a man who had protected and cared for her since the death of their parents. LooAnne hurt for Cathy but she could not take her mind off her own problems, things that had haunted her for her entire life and now that she had finally rid herself of them, they were arising anew!

When Belle Hall came into view LooAnne could not help the feeling inside her that longed to go home. However beautiful the hall was and no matter the warm welcome she had received, LooAnne wanted nothing more than to be in the safe embrace of her uncle. She knew she had to call him and tell him all that had occurred that morning but she could not risk that someone would overhear her again as Peter had.

The moment Mr. Andrews opened the large iron door for her she passed him quickly and climbed the stairs, desperate for a bit of solitude to sort out her thoughts.

The moment she shut her bedroom door LooAnne sighed, releasing a bit of stress from within her. She looked across the room, lit by the sunlight that streamed through the window at the far end, giving the room a soft glow. Slowly she walked towards it, her mind whirling with the events of the past hour. It had only been two days since she left home to continue her education, and yet it seemed as though it had been months. LooAnne's mind was lost in itself, the pain she felt inside and old feelings which had returned the moment she laid eyes on the man behind bars. A man who she should have known instantly, the moment she laid eyes on him at the train station, the moment he grabbed her to take her away. Why had she not realized then who he was? Why had she not recognized the feeling of his rough hands when he took hold of her as he had in years past?

"Years past," she whispered to herself. "Years I wished to forget."

LooAnne now stood in the warmth of the light that shown through the window. She stared at it until her eyes could bear it no longer and turned away only to meet them as they stared back at her in the full length mirror standing beside the bureau. She gazed at herself; looking deep within, she examined her inner most thoughts with great depth of feeling. LooAnne looked into her own eyes and recalled all the things they had seen, the tears they had cried, the times they had been thrown open with alert sense, and the times they had been shut tightly against the pain of the world; of her world, caused by her own family, one of them now a prisoner, separated from her only by the iron bars which she knew could not hold him for long! *What will I do?* she asked herself. *"Please, Lord,"* she prayed inwardly, *"don't let him find out. Don't let him know who I am. Please, protect me from my brother..."*

EIGHT

"I Know"

LooAnne stared at herself, her mind lost in times past and in fear of times to come. Never had her family been this close to finding out who she was and never had she been more afraid of the future. Why had her brother tried to take her? Why else then if he knew her true identity? And yet he said nothing on the matter and addressed her only as 'Miss Nash'. Did he not yet know who she really was? Had he tried to abduct her for another reason? LooAnne's mind was in quandary as to how and why; so many questions were unanswered and yet too many had been. LooAnne could feel her head pound with misunderstanding, her nerves wracked with fear, and her heart racing as though she had run for miles.

Her nerves were so wrought that LooAnne's heart leaped when she heard a soft knock at the bedroom door! She sighed and laid a calming hand on her chest before calling, "Come in."

The door was opened slowly and LooAnne assumed it to be Clara come to check on her but to her surprise the figure who stood in the doorway was not Clara but Peter. "Deputy Andrews," LooAnne's voice betrayed her shock at seeing him, though she hid her inward apprehension.

Peter nodded a greeting, his face calm but eyes full of question. "You left in a hurry, are you alright?" his question surprised LooAnne and she felt a small bit of warmth within her.

"Um, yes I'm fine. I just...don't like jails," she said, assuming that Peter, like most, would except the excuse, but to her dismay he didn't.

Peter frowned ever so slightly, his resolute stare locking on her face. "I know," he whispered.

"Y-you know what?" LooAnne asked, her nerves starting to tighten yet again.

Peter stepped into the room and closed the door behind him causing LooAnne to become defensive, "Excuse me, Deputy, but what exactly are you doing?" she demanded. Peter turned to her, his eyes searching her face for a reaction, "You know that fella, Miss Nash," he whispered. "I know you do."

LooAnne stepped back a bit, withholding a gasp. "W-what are you talking about?"

"The man in jail; You know who he is."

Peter's statement took LooAnne aback and she found herself at a loss for words. "I – I don't know what you're talking about, Deputy. I've never seen that man before in my life."

Peter shook his head, "You don't have to lie to me, Miss Nash. I won't tell anyone but I need to know who he is."

LooAnne shook her head and turned away from Peter, her emotions beginning to get the better of her and she could not understand why. Perhaps it was the way he looked at her, his eyes full of emotions she could not read, knowledge that she wished he didn't have. The way he confronted her with her past and his ability to look within her and draw out the truth.

"Miss Nash, I don't mean to hurt you. That's the last thing I wanna do but I gotta know who that man is," LooAnne could detect a bit of desperateness in the young deputy's voice. She took a deep breath, withholding the tears that threatened to spill.

"Why?" she whispered, turning to face him again. "Why do you need to know? Why can't you just put him behind bars for what he did and forget it?"

Peter sighed regretfully, "I know it's none of my business but I think there's more to this than we all realize."

"Of course there is!" LooAnne exclaimed. "My life! Mine and my uncle's! I know what you overheard yesterday and I thank you beyond your understanding for not saying anything but please forget it!"

"Miss Nash, I want to but I can't. I think this man might have something to do with Bill's murder!"

LooAnne's eyes widened. "W-what?"

"Tom told me after you left that the man who witnessed Bill's killing described the man we have behind bars!"

LooAnne gasped and shook her head in disbelief.

"The witness said he barely got a glimpse o' the killer as he was runnin' away, but he described a tall, muscular man with black hair, blue jeans and a ratty lookin' blue shirt. That describes this fella perfectly. I might be wrong but I at least gotta try. Bill was my friend since school, I can't let the man who killed him in cold blood get away with it. Please, Miss Nash, I don't want to hurt you or your uncle, but I gotta know his name."

LooAnne stared at Peter, tears pressing on the back of her eyes, a knot in her throat at the thought of Bill Morrison being shot down by a member of her own family...her brother. She didn't doubt his capability of such a heinous crime, knowing he had killed before, and yet to her this seemed much worse.

"His name..." LooAnne's voice came shaky and she paused to steady her breathing, "...is Cliff, Cliff Luther. He-he's my brother," LooAnne's voice cracked on the last word and she looked down, closing her eyes tightly, willing the tears not to fall.

She inhaled slowly but froze when she felt a gentle hand on her shoulder, sending small tingles down her arm which took her by surprise. LooAnne looked up into the face of Peter Andrews, his forever hard expression soft and sorrowful. "I'm sorry," he whispered earnestly.

LooAnne nodded, unable to remove her fixed gaze from his sea-blue eyes. "I know. It's not that I don't want him to pay for all he's done; he's committed so many atrocities to so many people, to me and my family, things he deserves to die for. I just can't imagine my brother being the one responsible for Bill's death." LooAnne turned away, Peter's hand leaving a warm, lasting print on her shoulder. "And to think he nearly had me the other day. I never imagined to see him again, I never wanted to see him again and yet he was so close to taking me! And he would have, if you hadn't stopped him." LooAnne looked over her shoulder and cast Peter a thankful smile. "I owe you my life, you know."

Peter nodded, "And I owe you mine."

LooAnne turned towards him again and shook her head, "Had it not been for me you wouldn't have needed any saving."

"You can't take responsibility for what your brother does," Peter said, keeping his voice its usual even tone. "But ya won't have to worry about him no more. He's behind bars where he belongs and if I can get evidence to prove it, he'll hang for what he did to Bill."

LooAnne sighed and looked at the ground. "If only it were that easy, Deputy, but I'm afraid it's not. I had four brothers you see, one was killed when the Luther's were driven from Decatur last year, one you have in jail, that means there are two more out there in the world somewhere, and if I know Luther's, those other two are not far behind the first. They stick together like glue and when they find out you've got Cliff in jail they won't be happy."

Peter frowned, "Would they try to break him out?"

LooAnne shrugged, "In days past they would have without a thought, but now that it's only them...I really don't know if they would or not."

"But you think they'll come after me for getting Cliff arrested?" Peter asked.

LooAnne nodded, "Almost sure of it. My brothers all took after my father, some more so than others. They're cruel, vile people, Deputy, people no one would want to deal with, and they don't take kindly to lawmen, especially when one's fought and taken one of them to prison."

"You mean I've made their list?" Peter added, sounding none too surprised.

LooAnne nodded grudgingly.

"Then the sooner this is all resolved the better."

"How do you plan on resolving it?" LooAnne questioned.

Peter sighed and shook his head, "I hope if I pressure your brother, he'll admit to the killing."

LooAnne shook her head and sighed, "That would never work I'm afraid. Luther's are trained to never snap even under the hardest of pressure. If he's determined not to tell you he won't."

Peter nodded, "I figured as much. There's gotta be some way to prove it was him."

"If it even was," LooAnne added.

Peter nodded, still in deep contemplation.

"Wait," LooAnne exclaimed, a thought donning on her, "Didn't Karen say she had seen the man talking with Bill?"

Peter's eyes instantly flew open and he nodded, looking more excited than LooAnne had ever seen him. "She did!" he exclaimed. "I bet she'd be able to identify him!"

"We couldn't do that to poor Karen though," LooAnne added wistfully.

Peter sighed and shook his head, "We ain't got much of a choice, Miss Nash."

"The poor girl has already been through so much; I hate to traumatize her further."

"So do I, but it might be the only way."

LooAnne nodded grudgingly. "I suppose you're right."

There was a moment of silence before Peter spoke again, looking at LooAnne intently. "You know I won't tell anyone."

LooAnne smiled gratefully at him, "Yes," she nodded, "I know you won't and I thank you so much for it."

"I should be the one thanking you. If you hadn't known who the fella was than I would be wrackin' my brain to find out."

LooAnne shrugged, "Even so, I wish I didn't know who he was."

Peter nodded, "In a way, so do I." With that he turned and opened the door, leaving the room without another word.

LooAnne stood in silence, staring after him, her shoulder still warm from where he had touched it, her mind more confused than ever before. Peter was a man, one of the only men alive, who knew of her secret and yet he did not pose a threat to her as she supposed he would. In her mind it was quite the opposite, she had wished before coming that she would not have to leave behind the only people who knew of her secret and could help and protect her but now, LooAnne realized, she had not left them all behind. Maybe she had the protection she had desired in the young deputy of Dallas County.

The rest of the afternoon passed without incident. Peter talked with Cathy about confronting the prisoner with what Karen had said and possibly getting the young girl to identify Cliff Luther as Bill's killer. As much as Cathy wanted the man who murdered her brother to pay for his crimes she was extremely reluctant to allow her sister to be forced into facing a man who may already be the one haunting her nightmares. She feared that in Karen's fragile state such a thing would cause her too much trauma to bear and she would descend back to the silent, terrified child she had been after Bill's death.
Peter resolved to give both Cathy and Karen time to recuperate from their brother's death before pressing the matter any further, not knowing that with every passing hour the Luther's grew closer and closer.
After her impassioned conversation with Peter, LooAnne had a light lunch and then set about calling her uncle to inform him of all the goings on. She made certain this time that no one was listening before asking the operator for the Nash Estate. Moments later she heard the voice of Chris Block who, after a cheerful greeting, said he would fetch her uncle.

LooAnne waited patiently until she heard her uncle's anxious voice on the line. "How did it go?" he asked almost immediately.

LooAnne looked about the entry hall once more before answering her uncle in a careful whisper. "Uncle Ricky, it-it's my brother! It's Cliff!"

"What? LooAnne are you sure?" Ricky's voice was full of both surprise and horror.

"I'm perfectly sure," LooAnne whispered, the tension in her voice beginning to grow.

"LooAnne, does he know who you are?"

"I – I don't know. I don't think he does otherwise he would have said something today in front of the police. And he called me Miss Nash, he didn't act as though he knew I was his sister but he might have been hiding it for one reason or another. Oh, Uncle Ricky, I don't know what to do. He tried to take me, I was almost kidnapped by my brother -"

"You need to come home, LooAnne," Ricky insisted immediately. "I know you haven't started classes yet but that can wait."

"I want to come home more than anything but you've gone to so much trouble and expense to get me here, I can't just leave now."

"LooAnne, your safety is more important than anything else and it's obviously compromised there. I'll arrange for you to return on the afternoon train from Dallas tomorrow."

Immediately an unwelcome feeling of sadness washed over her. How could she leave her new friends behind after they had done so much for her? And Peter; he had saved her life, learned her secret, and unknowingly comforted

95

her in a way even she could not discern. LooAnne suddenly felt a strange attachment to Dallas that she could not explain, an attachment which made her reluctant to leave.

"What would we tell everyone? What reason would we give?" she asked her uncle, a part of her hoping that he would not have an answer.

"Just tell them you're going home. Tell them you decided against college for now. There's no need to give anyone a good excuse."

Except that Peter will know the real reason, LooAnne thought, though she said nothing to her uncle, not wanting him to know that a total stranger knew their secret. "I suppose so," she agreed aloud.

"You sound uncertain, my dear."

"I just feel so silly," LooAnne admitted half the truth. "To come one day with plans of staying and going to school and then leave three days later. Everyone is bound to think me a fool."

"They'll do nothing of the kind. This has been a hassle since the beginning and now it's a threat to your safety. If you're here at least you can be better protected."

LooAnne nodded, though her uncle could not see her. "I know you're right, I just hate to drop everything for something that might not even happen."

"But do you want to take the chance that it will?" Ricky countered.

LooAnne sighed, "No, of course not. I guess I'll see you tomorrow then."

She could hear her uncle sigh before he spoke, "As much as I hate the situation we find ourselves in, I'll be very glad to see you, my dear."

LooAnne could not help but smile at this. "I'll be very glad to see you too, Uncle Ricky."

"I'll have your ticket ready and paid for at the station tomorrow afternoon. I love you, LooAnne."

"I love you too, Uncle Ricky. Goodbye."

"Goodbye."

LooAnne hung up the phone and sighed. As much as she longed to go home and be with her uncle she disliked the unwelcome feeling of sadness that compelled her to rethink her decision of departure. The fact that she wanted to stay at all took LooAnne quite by surprise as she had wanted nothing more than to be done with college and Dallas from the moment her uncle had decided to send her. But now it seemed she did not want to depart from her new found friends, or more particularly....*Peter Andrews.* LooAnne shook this thought from her mind, confused as to why she would care at all for leaving such a reticent man who had learned a precious secret due to eavesdropping. *I should be more upset over leaving Cathy and Clara.* LooAnne thought to herself.

She did not look forward to having to break the news of her departure to Clara, especially since she was the only one who knew of her secret suitor. This thought caused LooAnne's mind to wander to the elusive Stephen Parker. She wondered if Clara had heard anything regarding his whereabouts.

LooAnne decided that Clara would be the first to learn of her move back home so that she could ask the young maid about her ambiguous beau.

LooAnne headed upstairs to her room where she knew it would be safe to talk before ringing for her maid. Only a few moments passed before she heard a light knock at the door.

"Come in."

Clara entered immediately, "You rang for me, ma-am?" she asked.

"Yes, would you mind closing the door?"

Clara nodded and closed the door before turning questioning eyes on LooAnne.

"First of all," LooAnne began, "I'm afraid I won't be able to stay for my college classes. My uncle has gotten me a ticket and I'm leaving on the afternoon train tomorrow for Decatur."

Instantly Clara's face dropped a bit. "Oh, Miss Nash, why?"

LooAnne sighed, "I'm afraid it's a very complicated ordeal, Clara," she admitted.

"You mean cause of what happened yesterday?" the young maid guessed.

LooAnne nodded, "Not solely that, but yes, that's a part of the reason. My uncle thinks it's better if I come home and frankly so do I. He's all alone except for the staff and despite all the wonderful friends I've made here I need to be with him."

Clara nodded understandingly though she looked extremely sorrowful at the thought of LooAnne leaving. "I wish you didn't have to go, Miss Nash."

LooAnne smiled wanly, "So do I, Clara. But I'm afraid it can't be helped. I wanted to know though, before I go; how is everything between you and Stephen?"

Clara looked down at the carpet, not saying anything for a few moments but when she did it was evident she was trying to withhold her tears. "I – I haven't heard anything from him," she whispered, her voice full of sadness. "He –

he never came back after that night." Clara looked up at LooAnne her eyes filling with tears of hurt and regret. "Oh, Miss Nash, what if you were right? What if he doesn't intend to come back? What if he never even loved me?"

With this the young maid broke into tears, burying her face in her hands. LooAnne immediately went to her side, wrapping the poor girl in a comforting hug. She knew all too well what it was like to have a man pledge his love and loyalty, only to throw the girl away at the last minute.

"I'm so sorry, Clara," she whispered earnestly. "Maybe it's not as bad as you think? Maybe he couldn't make it?'

"I – I should have l-listened to you," Clara cried. "He-he never l-loved me. He's n-never gonna come b-back."

Clara's shoulders shook as she sobbed and LooAnne knew there was little she could say that would comfort her.

"Clara, you're a beautiful young woman and any man would be very lucky to call you his wife. There will be another, better man. One who deserves you."

Clara only sniffled and shook her head, "I don't want another man."

"I know, I felt the same way after my fiancé left me, I still do, but I know that no matter what, when God brings that man who He intended for me, I'll lose all the regret I have over Kyle because I'll be filled with love for the right one."

Clara pulled away from LooAnne and looked at her, her eyes red and her cheeks wet with tears. She sniffled a bit before saying, "Th-thank you for trying to help, Miss Nash, but – I just – I don't know what to think anymore."

LooAnne nodded, "I know, Clara, believe me I do. You know right after Kyle left Uncle Ricky told me something

I've thought about ever since then. He said 'He's out there, LooAnne, and he's one hundred times better than any other man in the world'. Ever since that day I've thought about those words. And my uncle was very right. I've not found that man yet, but when I do I'll know because he'll be one hundred times better than Kyle or any other man I've ever met. And you'll find your man too. This heartbreak you feel now will only make that man more special when he finally does come."

Clara had, by this time, stopped crying and now seemed to be going over LooAnne's words in her head. Finally, she looked up and said, "Is it wrong to miss Stephen, Miss Nash? Even after the way he's acted?"

LooAnne smiled and shook her head, "I still miss Kyle sometimes. Not the Kyle that lied to me and threw me aside for another woman, but the Kyle I thought he was before he showed his true character."

Clara nodded, "I suppose that's what I miss too. A part of me wants so badly to justify Stephen, like I can't admit to myself that he was just using me. I think part of me doesn't even believe it."

LooAnne cast Clara a wan smile and nodded, having felt the exact same way the following days after Kyle's departure. But now she realized, familiar feelings were beginning to take light deep within her, feelings she thought would not come to light for years. Feelings for another man...and LooAnne knew she had to fight them, or risk getting her heart broken again.

NINE

Taken Together

Clara began packing LooAnne's things while she went downstairs to inform Mrs. Andrews of the new arrangement. The housekeeper, though extremely disappointed, understood that LooAnne had only the best reasons for leaving. LooAnne told her much of what she had told Clara; that things had not worked out as planned and that she saw it best to return home. Mrs. Andrews expressed her sadness at LooAnne's departure but wished her well, telling her she would be sorely missed.

Cathy took the news extremely hard, however. Having just lost her brother and her sister being in a state of depression, the young woman was beside herself at the loss of LooAnne's company.

"Cathy, please, I promise to visit you as soon as all this is worked out," LooAnne vowed, trying to console her distraught friend.

Cathy sat on the end of her bed where Karen lay napping, her eyes glazed over with tears. "I know you will, but I'll miss you something awful, LooAnne," she sniffled.

"I'll miss you too, Cathy. I can't tell you how I wish I could be here for you, especially now, but my uncle is very right, it's best that I come home for the time being."

"I suppose it'd be nosy to ask why," Cathy said, though she looked at her friend questioningly.

LooAnne smiled kindly, "Of course not, Cathy. It's just that, ever since the beginning this has been nothing but a hassle and after what happened yesterday I just think it's best to call it a day and move on. But I promise I'll come back. I still need the education but things have just happened that prevent it from being now."

"You mean that fella attacking you, and Bill getting killed," Cathy asked though it was more of a statement.

LooAnne sighed and nodded. "Partly so. Oh, Cathy I honestly wish I could tell you the whole of it but there are some things that are just better left unsaid. I promise though, it has nothing to do with you or your brother. You were both very kind to me and if anything that makes it much harder for me to leave. I promise I'll come visit as soon as everything's cleared up."

Cathy smiled slightly, "You don't have to tell me everything, LooAnne. I know that some things are best left unsaid, but you will be badly missed, especially by me."

LooAnne gave Cathy a tight hug, all the while wondering how long it would be before she could return.

Later that evening LooAnne was busy packing when Mrs. Andrews knocked on her door saying there was a phone call for her. She hurried downstairs to the entry hall and picked it up. It was, as she had anticipated, her uncle, telling her that he had been able to get her a ticket for a train leaving the following morning at nine o'clock.

"If that's too early we can still reserve a seat on the twelve fifteen," he added.

"No that's fine, I'm nearly packed anyway."

"Alright, I've got to leave tonight for Austin for a business conference but I should be back in a couple of days, until then you stay inside. I've informed Chris of the situation and he'll look after you."

LooAnne nodded, "Alright, be careful."

"You too, my dear. I'll see you Wednesday then."

LooAnne smiled at the thought of seeing her uncle in a few days. "And I'm very glad for that at least. Goodbye, Uncle Ricky."

LooAnne could imagine her uncle smiling despite his inward worry. "I love you, my dear. You be careful too!"

"I will, Uncle Ricky, I promise. I love you too."

After their goodbyes LooAnne hung up and turned around only to see Peter Andrews approaching from the servant's quarters. His face was, as always, plain and impassive, but LooAnne thought she detected a bit of something else behind his bright blue eyes.

"You're leaving," he said, looking at her intently as he reached her side.

LooAnne nodded, searching him for the definition of the feeling she saw within him. "You of all people must know why."

"Because of him."

"Because of *them*. They'll come for their brother and then for me. Possibly you as well."

Peter shrugged as if this meant little to him. "I'm a lawman, that's what I signed up for."

LooAnne shook her head, "No man should have to sign up to deal with Luther's or anyone like them."

"But someone's gotta."

There was truth in Peter's words and it struck LooAnne hard. Someone, indeed, had to deal with the Luther's, but she found herself praying that it wasn't him.

"I'm sorry you might have to on my account," she responded.

Peter shook his head, "Don't make no difference. I'm glad I was there yesterday; I just wish I had had the chance to get him before he killed Bill."

LooAnne looked down, her heart aching at what her brother might have done. "So do I. I know it's terrible of me to say, but I wish someone had gotten to my brother a long time ago, all of them."

Peter looked at the floor for a moment before saying, "I have to get Karen to identify Cliff as Bill's killer so he can be tried for it as soon as possible. But Cathy won't let me even ask her."

"I don't blame her, Deputy, her sister is in a very fragile state and she's already been through too much as it is."

"I know, but we can't keep postponing the trial."

"But that man who saw the murderer running away, surely his word is enough to prove that Cliff did it?"

Peter shook his head, "It's not. He didn't see his face, only a glimpse of what he was wearing."

"So it might not have been Cliff?" LooAnne suggested.

Peter sighed and shrugged, "Bill was killed about a mile away from the place you were attacked, only thirty minutes before. Cliff had just enough time to kill Bill and then come for you."

LooAnne looked down and nodded. "I wish I knew why," she whispered. "I wish I knew why he killed Bill and why he tried to take me. I hope and pray he hasn't found out who I am."

"As long as he's behind bars he can't do anything," Peter pointed out.

"That's the thing, he might not be there for very long."

"We've got Cliff under twenty-four-hour guard so anyone who tries to take him should get the surprise of their life. But if we ever wanna get him tried for Bill's murder I have to get Karen to come identify him."

LooAnne sighed, knowing Peter was right, though she hated the idea of exposing the child to the very thing that had her so frightened.

"I wish there was another way, but we have to know," Peter added.

Suddenly an idea came to LooAnne and she looked at the young deputy excitedly. "Couldn't you take a photograph of Cliff and then show it to Karen?"

Peter's veiled expression instantly lightened at this new thought and for the first time LooAnne detected a hint of excitement on his face. "Yes," he nodded, the wheels in his head beginning to turn, "That's a wonderful idea. Please excuse me, Miss Nash" With that the young deputy turned and hurried out the front door looking extremely elated.

LooAnne smiled to herself, glad that her idea had made Peter so happy. She then turned and made her way upstairs to finish packing. She found Clara in her room, she had just finished packing some hat boxes and she smiled when she saw LooAnne. "I think these are the last of it, Miss Nash."

"Thank you, Clara, I appreciate it. I'll help you with the rest."

It only took another hour before LooAnne was entirely packed for her trip back home. She stared at the pile of boxes and suitcases, feeling a bit overwhelmed by it all. Her mind was so absorbed in the ordeal that she was startled when someone knocked lightly on her door. Clara opened it to reveal her mother.

"Miss Nash, there's a young man at the front door asking for you."

LooAnne immediately frowned, "Did he give you his name?"

The housekeeper shook her head, "No, he just said that he needed to talk to you as soon as possible."

LooAnne's frown deepened. "I can't imagine who it would be. I guess I'll go find out."

"He's waiting for you in the library."

LooAnne thanked Mrs. Andrews and made her way downstairs to the library which was just off the entry hall. She opened the wooden door and was instantly hit with the musty smell of books and pine wood. There was a man standing across the room looking out the window. His clothes were ragged and his curly hair mussed and unkept. When he heard LooAnne enter the young man turned around to face her, his familiar face taking LooAnne aback! They stared at each other, her in confusion and him in despondence. His face was dirty and there was a visible cut across his forehead as though he had been hit with something very hard. He held a torn hat in his cracking hands and his deep brown eyes looked at LooAnne as though he could see right through her.

Stephen Parker!

LooAnne recognized him instantly even from the quick glance she had gotten of him that night he ran from the house. But that was not the only bit of recognition that passed through her mind. For an instant LooAnne thought she had seen this young man somewhere before but dismissed the idea when she realized it was only because of their very brief meeting the night he came to see Clara.

Now she was at a loss to imagine what he would be doing here now, and why he wanted to see her.

"What are you doing here?" she asked, feeling nothing but dislike for the man who had hurt Clara as he had.

Stephen sighed and looked down at his hat. "Might as well get right down to it, Miss Nash," he stated factually. "I'm here on what ya might call a business matter."

"And what business matter would that be?"

The young man looked up at her, his eyes locking on her's. "I been sent for you, Miss Nash."

LooAnne instinctively took a step back, unsure how to respond to such a statement. "I'm afraid I don't know what you mean?"

"I'll make it real clear then," Stephen reached into his trouser pocket and pulled out a small mettle object, holding it in his hand for LooAnne to see. "You don't come with me and Peter Andrews is gonna die!"

LooAnne froze, a knot growing in her throat as she stared at the silver badge in Stephen's hand! She looked up at the man wide-eyed. "Who are you? Where's Deputy Andrews?"

"That ain't non o' your business, Miss Nash. And you make any sound to call for help and he's dead."

LooAnne nodded, assuring the man she would do as he asked.

"Now believe me I don't wanna do this," Stephen added, "but you either come with me or the family livin' in this house is gonna be down one member!"

Stephen's voice was uptight and threatening, as though this was something he had done before. LooAnne's heart was racing with worry for both herself and Peter! Who was this man? Why did he want her? Had he been after something much worse than using Clara the entire time? Had LooAnne been the reason he had gotten so close to her maid? And then the question foremost in her mind; what did he plan to do with her and the young deputy?

"Are ya comin' with me on your own or do I gotta force ya?"

LooAnne stood in shock for a moment before saying, "I'll go with you so long as you promise me no one will be harmed."

Stephen nodded, "Alright, here's how it's gonna be. You and me are gonna walk right out that font door to my truck and if someone tries to stop us you give 'em a good explanation or I'm gonna have to, you understand?"

LooAnne nodded, "And if we run into Clara?" she countered.

The expression on Stephen's face fumbled a bit before hardening. "You let me worry about that. Now get goin'."

"Why are you doing this?" LooAnne demanded.

"I can't tell ya, but you'll find out soon enough. No more talk, Andrews ain't got all day."

LooAnne restrained from commenting further and turned to exit the library, her heart beating wildly, mind racing with fear and uncertainty. Ordinarily she would do everything in her power to stop this man from taking her, but Peter had already risked his life for her once, she had no intention of having him lose it because she was afraid. She walked as calmly as she could towards the big iron front door, looking throughout the downstairs for any member of the staff who might question her leaving; but she saw no one and silently thanked God that Clara was not here. LooAnne knew nothing of Stephen Parker or his intentions towards her and Clara. She assumed that he had been using Clara to get to her but the twinge of sorrow in his eyes when she had mentioned the young maid caused her to wonder otherwise.

The moments that passed between the library and the front door were grueling; LooAnne took hold of the knob but froze, fear of what was to come causing her stomach to turn. She wanted with all her being to call out for the staff to come and stop this man from taking her to an unknown location for unknown reasons. She knew very well that they could as he did not appear to be armed and would more than likely make a run for it should LooAnne call out for help. But then she thought of Peter, the innocent young deputy who she had unintentionally pulled into the complications of her life, she could not let him die for her, and this thought was what compelled LooAnne to turn the knob and walk from the safety of Belle Hall towards an old Model T parked on the road just outside the gate. LooAnne could feel Stephen Parker's presence close behind her, no doubt keeping a keen eye open for anyone who might try to stop them. She walked as slowly as she could, unsure of what she expected to come of it but dreading the moment she was no longer free but in the hands of a man who she knew meant her harm.

When they reached the automobile Stephen opened the rear door and told LooAnne to get in. Again she paused but not for long as she caught sight of an unconscious Peter Andrews sprawled across the back seat! LooAnne leaped in and instantly went to his aid. His forehead was bleeding from where he had been struck, knocking him into his present state! LooAnne did her best to get him into a sitting position as Stephen climbed in the driver's seat and took off down the road.

"What did you do to him!" LooAnne demanded angrily.

"He's just unconscious," Stephen defended, keeping his eyes on the road in front of him.

"Well, you have me now so let him go!" LooAnne's voice was demanding, as though she expected this man to heed her words.

"I can't," was all he said.

"Why not? You've used him to get me, surely you can't need him for anything else."

"That ain't my decision."

This answer surprised and worried LooAnne. It meant that Stephen was not the only one in on this scheme, there was someone else!

"Well who's is it then?"

Stephen didn't answer right away but when he did LooAnne wished that she had never inquired. "*Will Luther.*"

LooAnne gasped and fell back in her seat a bit, her eyes wide with fear! Will Luther; Cliff's twin brother! One of the worst Luther's LooAnne had ever known!

"I told ya not to ask questions," Stephen spoke, seeing how this information had jarred his prisoner.

LooAnne sank back in the seat next to Peter, her heart striking her chest so hard she felt as if she might lose consciousness herself. Did her brothers know who she was? If not, then why would they want to kidnap her? *Perhaps to get revenge on Uncle Ricky,* she thought. The Nash's and Luther's had been arch enemies, ever since Ricky's grandfather first made his fortune and moved to Decatur. The Nash's had been nothing but a threat to the Luther's. Two great powers living side by side, as their land bordered to the south, they had forever been out to

110

destroy the other.

LooAnne's mother's elopement had wreaked havoc, her marriage to Jason Luther being a tie between the enemies that none could sever, and the main reason LooAnne and her brothers had been hated by their family for the Nash blood they carried. Her brothers had learned quickly that they could earn their family's respect by becoming everything they were. LooAnne however, refused to be like them, a decision which resulted in abuse and hatred. And now she feared she would be forced back into that life she had escaped from so many years before!

LooAnne knew she had to get a hold of herself. She would not be able to think clearly should her mind go into a panic. LooAnne took a deep breath and whispered a prayer before asking, "What does Will Luther want with me? I've done nothing to him!"

"That ain't the way he sees it," Stephen answered. "He says you and your uncle were the ones who got half the Luther's killed in Decatur last year."

LooAnne thought back to the previous summer when the small town had been forced to fight the Luther family, most of whom had been killed. She recalled how she and her uncle had, indeed, been the source of their ruin. *They are after revenge then,* LooAnne thought. *There's no telling what they'll do!*

For a moment LooAnne contemplated an attempt to jump from the vehicle and try to get away but she could not leave Peter and he most certainly was not in any condition to escape with her. LooAnne knew there was nothing she could do until he awoke, she only prayed that it wouldn't be too late.

Stephen drove for quite a few miles down roads LooAnne

was unfamiliar with. He had long since left the city of Dallas and appeared to be driving north-west towards Decatur, over sixty miles from the city but, to LooAnne's delight, closer to home!

It had been nearly an hour and LooAnne was beginning to worry about Peter who still had not awakened, when Stephen pulled off the road in a rural area not far from the Dallas city limits.

"What are we doing?" LooAnne demanded, a feeling of apprehension coming over her.

"Pickin' up Will," were Stephen's words that caused LooAnne to sink back in her seat. She knew that showing her fear would only cause her more harm, but there was nothing that scared her more than being face to face with her brother!

Stephen stuck his head out of the car and called, "Will! I got 'em!"

Moments later LooAnne caught sight of her oldest brother emerging from within the thicket. Though not identical to his twin, Will was quite similar to Cliff with the same dark down eyes, black hair, and grizzled face. He reminded LooAnne of her fading memory of their father, tall and broad with a hard expression ever present on his scarred face. Will still bore his signature scar on his right cheek from a raid when the Luther's were in their prime. He had been grazed by a bullet and wore the proof of his escape proudly. LooAnne could not help but wish that Peter were awake now that she was faced with one of the most vile Luther's still alive!

"Did ya have any trouble?" Will asked, his voice low and hard.

Stephen shook his head, "No, she came along easy once I

had Andrews."

Will opened the passenger door and looked in the back, an evil smile growing instantly on his face.

"Well, well, well, if it ain't Miss LooAnne Nash."

"W-what do you want with me?" LooAnne asked, trying her best to hide her fear.

"You were the reason my family was killed in Decatur last year," Will sneered. "And now I intend on makin' you and your uncle pay for it!"

"Then let the deputy go!" LooAnne demanded. "He's got nothing to do with this."

"He took my brother," Will stated factually, "and no second rate lawman messes with me and mine."

"He only did it to save me, it was my fault, please let him go!" LooAnne was unsure as to why she was so worried for Peter Andrews. They had only known each other two days and yet for some reason she felt very close to him and was not about to let her wicked older brothers hurt him because of something she had done.

"Listen, Missy, you don't argue with me and you don't tell me what to do! I hear another word outta your mouth and it'll be the last you ever speak! Understand?"

LooAnne knew there was nothing to do but keep silent if she ever wanted to free herself and Peter. She looked over at his unconscious body beside her, blood plastered to the side of his face, she imagined how Bill had been shot down in cold blood, his sister's left to bear the scar of his death forever.

Looking at her brother she remembered how he had bullied her until she ran away; how he had shoved her, hit her, tattled on her, made her do his chores day after day, told her how little she was loved, how she would never be worth the air she breathed. LooAnne could no longer stand being in his presence. However far-fetched it was LooAnne could no longer think clearly as she made a rash decision. Without another word she turned and yanked open the door, flying from the vehicle as Stephen fumbled with his door and Will yelled out in anger!

LooAnne had no idea where she was going but she knew she had to get away! Maybe if she could she would be able to send help back for Peter! *What am I thinking?* part of her mind cried out as she ran. *I can't leave him! They'll kill him!* And yet another part urged her on! Praying that she would be able to reach help before anything could happened to the young deputy!

LooAnne could hear her captors behind her, hot in pursuit of their lost prisoner! She dodged and leaped branches, fighting her way through the thick woods, knowing that Will and Stephen were not far behind! She had not gone far however before Will's voice called, "Stop right there or Peter Andrews dies!"

LooAnne's first instinct was to disregard the threat and keep running but with every step she took she knew that the likelihood of Peter being killed was great. *I can't let him die because of me,* she told herself. *He deserves to live his own life, not die because of mine!*

This thought slowed LooAnne's pumping legs until they were at a standstill. She stood, panting helplessly in the midst of the woods waiting to be seized by her brother's angry grip. Moments later he reached her, yanking her around to face him as he brought an angry hand down on her face! The force caused LooAnne to fall to the ground where her head struck a large rock! Seconds later her left eye was blinded by a flow of blood and the trees before her began to rapidly fade.

"Will, that's enough!"

"Stay outta this, Ben!" Were the last words she heard before darkness overtook her!

TEN

Stories of a Lifetime

LooAnne didn't know how long she had been unconscious, nor what had happened while she was. She didn't know where she had been taken, who she was with, or what had happened to Peter. All she could feel was the endless pounding of her head and the hard floor beneath her as she started to come too.

She felt a moist bit of cloth on her forehead, easing the searing pain that pulsed throughout her temple. Slowly she was able to open her eyes only to be faced with the foggy form of a man hovering over her. She felt the cloth being lifted from her head as she moaned and laid a weak hand on her face.

"Miss Nash?" LooAnne recognized Peter's voice immediately and was instantly relaxed by the sound of it. "D-Deputy," she groaned as his handsome face cleared and she could see his blue eyes directly above her, filled with concern.

And then she remembered...Stephen Parker, being taken away, Peter's unconscious state, and her brother! These thoughts caused her heart to speed up again as she tried to sit only to have the pain in her head wash over her.

"Easy, Miss Nash," Peter spoke as his large hands gently eased her shoulders back against the floor. "Lay still, you hurt your head pretty bad."

LooAnne sighed and laid back feeling the hard floor beneath her head. She closed her eyes for a moment before curiosity overtook her.

"W-where are we?" she asked.

Peter sighed as though he didn't want to tell her. "I'm not exactly sure, but I think it's the Luther Estate."

At this LooAnne was sitting in a flash, ignoring her aching head as adrenalin shot through her! She moved away from Peter and looked around frantically only to feel her heart sink as she recognized her surroundings!

The house she had been born in, the house she grew up in, the house where she had last seen her mother and father alive; where she had hidden from her ruthless family, where she had listened to their drunken brawls and hateful words, where she had spent many sleepless nights praying that somehow it would all end. Memories flooded LooAnne and in an instant she was overcome with them! She buried her face in her hands, pulling her knees to her chest as she tried to calm her breathing. However she willed the tears to come they would not, she was forbidden to cry in this place, knowing it would only bring more pain.

LooAnne was lost within the terrors of her mind until she felt the gentle, familiar hand of Peter Andrews on her shoulder.

"It's alright," his even voice whispered. "We'll get out, I promise." he seemed to be at a loss for words but LooAnne found herself comforted by his presence alone. *Stop it, LooAnne! You can't get attached to another man!*

117

Her mind scolded, though she knew this was no time to worry about matters of the heart when their lives were in danger. She took a deep breath, trying to recompose herself as she lifted her head from her knees. She closed her eyes for a moment as her nerves began to calm, then she looked up into Peter's worried face.

"I'm sorry," she whispered, still trying to retain control of her breathing.

Peter shook his head, "Don't be sorry. Are you alright?"

LooAnne swallowed hard and nodded, "Yes, are you?"

"I'm fine."

LooAnne's eyes wandered to the deputy's forehead which showed a large knot from where he had been hit. It was bruising badly but the bleeding had long since stopped.

"I'm so sorry I got you drug into this," she apologized, staring at Peter dolefully.

The deputy shook his head, "None of this is your fault, Miss Nash. You can't help what these people do."

LooAnne sighed and laid her head back against the wall, taking in the familiar room she had not seen in nearly seven years. It was clear of furniture but an abundance of dust and cob webs covered the walls, floors, and dark corners. There was a single window at the far end of the room, it's glass broken and panes severed revealing the sight of treetops from the second story, allowing the afternoon light to fill the dim room.

Slowly LooAnne started to get to her feet only to face Peter's immediate protests.

"I'm alright," she insisted, casting him a kind smile.

He helped her to her feet, steadying her until she was able to regain her balance. LooAnne thanked him and then slowly made her way across the room to look out the window at the overgrown yard and trees beyond. Drifts of broken wood lay at the base of the house where they had come lose and fallen, branches and young saplings cluttered the yard hiding broken whiskey bottles that had been carelessly discarded, left for the weeds and grass to overtake them. LooAnne could not see far for the thick woods that surrounded the large house, once a beautiful estate, now left to ruin.

She gazed at the familiar land before her, memories she thought she had forgotten forevermore flooded her mind as she recalled the days of her early childhood.

"I never should have left here," she whispered to herself though not quiet enough that Peter Andrews didn't hear. He straightened from his crouched position on the floor behind her and was about to speak when the creaking of the floorboards in the hall was heard as someone approached the door!

LooAnne felt her muscles tense and her heart race! Peter whirled around, ready to face his captor with whatever strength he had!

Moments later the lock clicked and the door swung open revealing the broad frame of Will Luther! But he was not alone; to both LooAnne and Peter's surprise he was accompanied by Stephen Parker who was bound and gagged!

Will threw Stephen to the floor where he landed with a painful thud, unable to catch himself with his restricted hands.

Peter and LooAnne stared at the sight in confusion, their minds unsure of what to make of the situation.

Will wore a satisfied smirk on his face as he stepped into the room, gun barrel displayed before him to keep his prisoners back!

"Thought I'd bring ya some company," he stated. Then smiled at the looks of misunderstanding on his prisoners' faces. "Oh, you thought he was with me?" Will continued arrogantly. "Well think again. I've had enough o' this moron bein' a thorn in my side!" With that he backed out of the room, slamming the door behind him!

The room was plunged into silence as LooAnne and Peter looked first at each other then at Stephen Parker who immediately began pulling at the ropes that bound him, mumbling incoherently through the cloth in his mouth. After a moment's pause Peter knelt by his side and pulled the cloth from his mouth, casting it aside.

"Thanks," Stephen said hoarsely, licking his dried lips, "untie me will ya?"

Peter shook his head as he rose back to his feet, "I don't think so. Not until you tell us what exactly is goin' on."

Stephen sighed, "Look I know you two don't trust me and -"

"And we got every right not to!" Peter informed him, irritably.

"I know you do, but I swear I didn't want any part o' this! I even tried to talk Will out of it."

"You tried to talk him out of it but when he wouldn't you decided to help him?" Peter countered.

"Of course not!" Stephen continued to struggle against the ropes. "Look could you at least get me off the floor?"

Peter thought a moment then sighed in agreement and helped the bound man sit against the wall.

"Now start explainin'," he commanded.

Stephen looked from Peter to LooAnne and then let his gaze fall to the floor and nodded, "I guess I should start at the beginning, but I want y'all to know that I ain't like Will or any other Luther for that matter. This wasn't my idea and I really did try to stop them."

"You're talkin' about Will and Cliff I suppose?" Peter asked.

Stephen nodded. "They been out to get the Nash's ever since we were run from Decatur last year."

"What do you mean *we*?" LooAnne spoke for the first time and Stephen looked up at her, his eyes filled with remorse.

"Miss Nash, I really am sorry Will hit you. I swear I tried to stop him."

"Answer my question, Stephen," LooAnne demanded, her mind whirling with an assortment of possibilities as to how this young man fit in with the Luther's.

Stephen sighed and let his gaze fall back to the dirty wood floor. "First of all my name ain't Stephen Parker, I changed it so I could..." Stephen stopped, glancing up at Peter who stood over him watchfully.

"So you could what?" the young deputy asked.

"So I could – um -"

"So you could go out with Clara Andrews," LooAnne finished for him.

At mention of his sister Peter's eyes grew wide, "What!" he exclaimed, anger beginning to grow inside him.

"You've been doing what with my sister?"

"I've been courting her ever since I saved her from Will last year," Stephan admitted.

Peter grabbed hold of Stephen's shirt collar angrily.

"What're you talkin' about? I swear if you hurt my sister I'll kill you!"

Stephen tensed, his face only inches away Peter's. "I

didn't! I've been nothin' but a gentleman toward your sister! We're all in this mess right now because I was tryin' to protect her!"

Peter pulled back his fist and was about to hit Stephen when LooAnne grabbed it and restrained him. "Deputy, please! That won't help anything. At least let the man explain?"

Peter looked back at LooAnne and reluctantly lowered his fist, releasing Stephen from his hold as he did. "Fine, but you better have a good explanation for all this!"

LooAnne had never seen Peter so angry. His usual calm and reserved personality had disappeared at mention of this man going out with his sister behind his back and for some reason it caused LooAnne to admire the young deputy even more.

"I would advise you to start at the beginning and explain everything to us, Stephen," LooAnne urged.

The young man nodded and said, "I guess the beginning was last year when most of the Luther's were either killed or taken to jail because of you and your uncle, Miss Nash. It made the remaining Luther's so angry, they vowed to get revenge on you both and have been plotting it ever since. We've been living here in Dallas ever since last year and when they heard you would be comin' to Dallas for college Will and Cliff saw it as the perfect time to take you and then use you to force your uncle to either give us money or his life."

"Wait," LooAnne stopped Stephen before he could go on, feeling a knot beginning to grow in her throat as she put together all the pieces in her mind. "You-you said your name wasn't Stephen Parker. You-you're a – a Luther...aren't you?"

Stephen looked at the ground, shame on his face, and nodded slowly. "I am," he admitted quietly. "My name's Ben..."

At mention of her twin brother's name LooAnne took a step back and turned away from the two men, scenarios from a lifetime playing over in her mind. Running with her brother through the fields, doing the chores he was too weak to do, holding him close at night when he cried, protecting him from their cruel relatives, loving him when there was no one else to love.

He had been born unhealthy and weak, for years their mother feared he wouldn't make it through another winter, but with his only sister's forever watchful eye and protective hand he had slowly begun to grow stronger despite the cruelty that surrounded them. But the reality of the situation struck LooAnne like a knife to the chest. *"I left him,"* she thought, *"I left him here to face the Luther's alone. I should have known he wouldn't grow up to be like them. Why didn't I take him away with me?"*

And then she remembered the so recent words of Karen Morrison as she wept in Dave's arms. *"He-he said he would take me. The man – came to s-see Bill. He said he w-would k-k-kill Bill and t-take me a-away if Bill didn't t-tell him."*

"Tell him what, Butterfly?"

"Where Ben is."

Ben...

And that was when LooAnne understood the reason Bill had been killed and she could not withstand the reality any longer. Despite her attempts to withhold her emotions, the sight of her twin brother and the fact that she might have prevented all of this caused LooAnne's strong barrier to break, allowing floods of tears to overflow. LooAnne cupped a restraining hand over her mouth in an attempt to muffle her sobs, feeling the eyes of her brother and Peter on her back. She was beyond wishing she had never left the estate, beyond the fear of what would happen to her and Peter; all LooAnne wished now was that she had never left the Luther's, that she had never been born. Though only a few seconds had passed it felt like an eternity before a pair of unfamiliar arms wrap around her crying frame. She knew instantly that they were Peter's; his strong, toned arms holding her close, encasing her body in a warmth she had never felt before, a warmth that calmed her.

Despite her inward protests LooAnne buried her face in the deputy's uniform, returning his embrace as her tears continued to flow. *He knows,* she realized. H*e knows Stephen is my brother.* And though in days past she had feared Peter's knowledge of her Luther blood, she now took comfort in it, knowing that he understood part of the reason for her tears.

All remained silent until LooAnne's cries slowed. Peter never moved nor said a word, he made no attempt to console her other than his tight embrace which she found was all she needed. LooAnne inhaled his now familiar scent before stepping out of his arms, inwardly scolding herself as she viciously wiped at the tears in her eyes with the cuff of her blouse sleeves.

"I – I'm sorry," she whispered, sniffling a bit. "I – I didn't mean -"

"Don't apologize," Peter insisted, his eyes watching her carefully. "It's alright."

"Miss Nash, I'm sorry. I know how y'all feel about being

related to us but-"

"No it's fine," LooAnne interrupted Stephen, composing herself as best she could. "But you have to tell us.... were you the reason Bill Morrison was killed?"

Peter instantly took on a look of confusion as Stephen looked at the ground and nodded.

"How?" Peter demanded, his dislike for Stephen Parker growing by the minute.

"When me and my brothers and cousin ran from Decatur I got separated from them and ended up here in Dallas." Stephen began. "I lived on the street for a couple weeks lookin' for a job. I saw one mornin' that the bank windows needed cleaning and thought maybe the manager would pay me enough to get somethin' to eat if I washed 'em. That was when I first met Bill, he was a great fella and when he saw how much I needed the money he let me, no questions asked. After that he kept givin' me odd jobs around the bank and tending to his yard. I was finally eatin' good and could start saving up for room and board somewhere. I'd told Bill my name was Stephen Parker and I had no family which I thought was true enough, and he helped me every way he could. Even got me the job at the mill. After that I was able to get a room at a boardinghouse not too far from Belle Hall. Everything was goin' really good and I considered Bill the only friend I've ever had. I was finally away from being bullied by my family and could start new. I worked at the mill for about a year and I thought things were finally lookin' up for me until Bill showed up one mornin' about a week ago lookin' right angry. He took me aside and said that my brothers had been to his house lookin' for me. Bill said that when he told 'em he didn't know any Ben Luther they had gotten mad and threatened to hurt him and his sisters if he didn't tell 'em were I was."

"That must've been what Karen over-heard," Peter interrupted. "When she was saying the fella said he would take her away, she must've been there when Will and Cliff threatened Bill!"

LooAnne nodded slowly, wrapping her mind around all the new developments and the fact that it was now certain one of her brothers had killed Bill Morrison.

"Keep going," she urged Stephen.

The young Luther nodded and continued, "I gotta admit I was scared. I never wanted anything more to do with Will and Cliff and thought I had managed to lose 'em for good only to find out they were still in Dallas and had threatened the man who had more or less saved my life just sent me over the edge. I couldn't lie to Bill anymore so I told him everything right there on the spot. I thought he would hate me, I just knew he was gonna go right up to my employer and tell him to fire me but he didn't. He patted me on the shoulder and said 'Well don't worry, kid, I won't tell them where you are'." Stephen shook his head sadly, staring off into nothing as he recalled the events after that. "I tried to warn Bill, I tried to tell him my brothers would carry out any threat they used. I told him it was best to just tell 'em what they wanted but he said he wasn't gonna do that to me."

"Well they obviously found you anyway," LooAnne commented.

Stephen nodded, "They'd followed Bill that day knowing he would try to talk to me at some point. Once they knew where I was they couldn't leave Bill alive to tell the sheriff that there were Luther's in town and that they had threatened him..."

"So they killed him," Peter finished solemnly.

Stephen nodded, "Cliff shot him down in cold blood."

"But how did Will and Cliff know you were in Dallas and that Bill could tell them where?" LooAnne questioned, still a bit confused.

Stephen glanced up at Peter for a moment before saying, "Not too long before I met Bill at the end o' last summer I was out lookin' for work. I heard someone scream from across the street and looked over to see some guy gettin' rough with a girl...your sister, Andrews."

LooAnne saw Peter tense but he made no move to stop Stephen as the young Luther went on. "I stopped him before she could get hurt, not realizing it was Will until it was too late. He recognized me and was so mad he hit me in the face, that was when we both saw you come runnin'. Neither of us knew you were her brother, just that you were a lawman so we hightailed it outta there. I was able to get away from Will and thought that if I laid low for a bit he'd forget about me and go on his way. He never liked me anyway and I figured he'd be glad to get me outta his hair. And I did manage to stay away from him for nearly an entire year before he went to Bill lookin' for me. I know it was stupid to think I could lose 'em forever, knowing my brothers they would never allow me to take all my Luther secrets outside the family, but at the time I couldn't think o' nothin' but that beautiful girl."

"*My* little sister!" Peter sneered.

Stephen nodded, having no intention of denying it now. "I ran into her again not long after that and we got acquainted. She was – is – the most beautiful, sweet-natured girl I've ever met. I wanted to court her proper but

I knew I couldn't force my life on her, she deserves better than me but at the time I was just so amazed that any girl would take to me the way she seemed to that I wasn't thinkin' about how it might hurt her if Will and Cliff found out."

"And they did," LooAnne added.

Stephen nodded, "The day you came, Miss Nash, the day before Bill was killed, Cliff was comin' to get me from the boardinghouse, to take me to wherever he and Will were stayin', and saw me and Clara together. Luckily I saw him too and sent her home telling her I'd come talk to her that night. Ever since that day he's used her to get me to do anything they want. After Cliff got caught the first time he tried to take you, Miss Nash, Will came up with the plan o' takin' Deputy Andrews and using him to get you. He wanted to break Cliff out but saw that it would be too risky so instead he decided to get revenge on Andrews for arrestin' him. He said if I didn't help him he'd hurt Clara just like he had Bill."

Stephen looked up at his listeners despondently. "I didn't want to help him, honest I didn't. I tried to talk him out of it but he said he'd take Clara instead. I knew he was capable of doing anything and I couldn't let him. Now this is all my fault." Stephen bent his head in shame, unable to face the two he had swapped for a girl he loved.

"And you did come that night," LooAnne added. "That was the night I caught you and Clara in the entry hall." Stephen nodded. "I'd slipped away while Will and Cliff were asleep. I wanted her to run away with me and get married."

"You wanted what!" Peter exclaimed.

"Look I know it was wrong but she wasn't safe and neither

128

was I!" Stephen defended himself. "I was, and still am, in love with her! I knew I would never get another chance once Will and Cliff realized I was gone. It was run away with her or without her...or at least I thought it was. Turns out Will had woken up when I left and followed me to see what I was doin'. When Miss Nash caught me and Clara I ran off the grounds right into him. He was plenty mad too, that's how I got this," Stephen pointed to the cut over his eye. "But I didn't care at that point. I loved Clara and lost her forever to a life I thought was behind me. Now I'll never get her back, heaven only knows what she thinks o' me."

LooAnne turned and gazed out the window, unable to find the right words to say. How could she explain to this young man, her own brother, that she was his lost sister who had abandoned him for the chance of freedom? How could she tell him that she was just as much responsible for what had happened as he was?

Peter stood still for a moment, his outward expression calm but his mind whirling, before bending down to untie Stephen Parker.

He loosened the bonds and looked Stephen in the eye, "Well, now that we all know the truth, we're gonna get outta here. And you're gonna help."

Stephen looked up and frowned as LooAnne turned questioning eyes on the deputy. "How?" they asked in unison.

"You step one foot into that hallway and my brother will kill you before you make it out the front door," Stephen warned.

Peter straightened from the floor and said, "Is Will the only one out there?"

Stephen shook his head, "Ray, our cousin, is out there with him, he's been in on it from the start."

"And they're the only two?"

Stephen nodded, "Yeah, they plan on usin' Miss Nash to get Cliff outta jail as soon as they get their hands on her uncle."

"When will that be?" LooAnne asked anxiously.

"Tomorrow morning."

"Then we've got to get out of here before that!" LooAnne exclaimed.

Peter nodded stiffly, "We will."

ELEVEN

Running!

As night began to fall LooAnne, Peter, and Stephen heard nothing from the first floor below them, though they knew Will and his cousin could not be far away.
While locked in their makeshift prison the threesome had concocted a plan of escape, and now all that was left was a fervent prayer that it worked!
Until then they lay in silence, each trying to get all the rest they could, bettering their chances to get away come the morning. Peter and Stephen had positioned themselves by the door just in case Will appeared during the late hours, but as the night went on there was nothing to be heard but the chirp of crickets and frogs outside the broken window.
LooAnne stood quietly in front of it, her mind and body unable to sleep as she leaned against the window pane and stared into the moonlit sky. A cool breeze blew in from the fields, carrying the pure smell of the countryside.
LooAnne closed her eyes as she inhaled it, for a moment imagining that things were different, that she was not at her old home being held prisoner by her psychotic brother and cousin but that she was home at the Nash Estate.
Home, LooAnne thought as she gazed out over the dark trees. Though she could not see it, LooAnne knew that her

uncle's land was only a few miles from where she was now held. She could almost see it there, offering her freedom just as it had seven years before when she had run away. Just knowing that her home was not far gave a certain peace to LooAnne's heart, knowing that come morning, if all went well, she could lead her friends to that same freedom where the Lord had led her many years before. LooAnne opened her eyes and sighed, being met with the same darkness of the Luther Estate, a darkness she longed to run away from. Memories had not ceased to haunt her since the moment she had awakened a prisoner in her old home. With every turn she made a picture of the past could be seen; she could see her mother moving throughout the room with grace and calmness. She could see her father throwing open the door to yell at her and her brothers or to lay down on his bed without a word to any of them. She remembered the endless days of working and training only to be kept awake at night by the angry yelling of her family as her mother sat by her side, never once saying a word. Though the bad memories came in abundance LooAnne could also recall the good ones. The times when she and her mother would run out to pick the first spring flowers, the hours they would spend devoted to LooAnne's schooling, the days her father would come in and smile at her or catch her up in his arms as she ran in from the fields.

"What ya been about, Bethy?" he would say, his usual strained, angry voice, for some reason content and happy. LooAnne smiled at this memory, realizing how much she actually missed her parents. At the time of their death she had been so angry at them for leaving her alone to protect herself and her brother from the rest of their family, but as

time had gone on her love for them slowly became more and more evident to her. And though they, especially her father, had not shown it, their love for her became more apparent as well.

This thought reminded LooAnne of the night her father had died. Of how he had been brought back from town badly wounded by the bullet of an innocent man trying to protect himself and his belongings. LooAnne looked back from the window and could picture her uncles coming through the bedroom door and laying her barely conscious father on his bed which had sat not far from where she stood now. LooAnne remembered running to them, asking desperately for her mother only to be told that she had been killed and was not coming back!

LooAnne remembered watching as the family did everything they could to save her father but it was of no use. By the time midnight fell they had given up their attempts at saving him, leaving her to sit by his side while he died. LooAnne knew that no matter how long she might live; she would never forget those last moments...

"Your mother was right," Jason Luther breathed unsteadily as he addressed his nine-year-old daughter who sat on the bedside watching him slip away. "I should o' taken y'all away from here a long time ago."

"We can go when you're better, Papa," she assured him, though they both new that day would not come.

"No, Bethy," he shook his head, "I can't go. I'm gonna go be with your Mama."

The child shook her head as she thought about her father leaving her as her mother had. "But you can't! You can't leave me with them!"

"N-now there'll be no argument, child," her father

scolded.

"But what will Ben and me do, Papa?"

Jason sighed and looked at the ceiling above him, thoughts of his wasted life running through his dying mind. Finally, he turned and looked at his only daughter. "Ya gotta get outta here, Beth," he whispered hoarsely. "Ya gotta get out..."

"Miss Nash, you alright?" Peter's deep Texan drawl freed LooAnne of her thoughts, startling her a bit as she was brought back to the present. It was only then that she realized Peter was awake and standing not too far from her.

"Oh, I'm sorry, yes," she nodded. "I'm perfectly fine." LooAnne could not see the deputy's expression in the dark but she distinguished his stiff nod as he walked to her side and looked out the window at the night. "Can't sleep?" he asked.

LooAnne looked down and shook her head, "I never could sleep in this place," she whispered quietly, not wanting Stephen to awaken and overhear.

Peter nodded and remained silent for a moment, his eyes falling from the window to LooAnne's dark figure beside him. She could feel his gaze on her and looked up, meeting the moonlight that reflected off his blue eyes. He stared at her as though he could see right into her soul, as though he were trying to read her mind like an open book, wondering what things he would find there.

LooAnne met the gaze of the mysterious deputy, her too searching for something she did not yet know she looked for; something she inwardly longed for. No longer could she forget the feelings she had experienced the moment she saw the young deputy standing opposite her attacker, ready to risk his life to save her. *You can't fall for this man, LooAnne Nash!* she inwardly scolded herself. *Do you not remember how Kyle treated you? It's too soon to risk your heart again.* And yet she could not seem to take her eyes off his. No matter how her mind scolded her, LooAnne could no longer disregard the way her heart leaped when he spoke to her, the way she admired his rugged, yet gentle masculinity, and the way his warm embrace had calmed her even in the worst of circumstances.

Peter stared at her unwavering, his face lit slightly by the moon. Never had he been so taken with a young woman. So lost in her that his mind could dwell on nothing else. He yearned to tell her how he felt for her, to express the feelings he had bottled up within him from the moment he first saw her struggling in the arms of her brother. Never had he been so shocked to learn anything as he had when overhearing her confess her true identity. How could such a beautiful, kind girl be the offspring of a Luther, he had asked himself. How could the well-known niece and heiress of Rick Nash be the runaway daughter of a killer and thief?

These thoughts had, at first, been a cause for doubt and suspicion in the young deputy's mind. Yet the more he had talked with her, the more Peter had gotten to know both sides of her complicated life, the more he adored her ability to live them both.

"You should be asleep," LooAnne's whisper cut into Peter's thoughts and he realized how silent they both had been.

"So should you."

LooAnne sighed and looked at the floor where Stephen lay, allowing her gaze to part with Peter's. "I can't," she admitted. "There are too many things to think about."

"You mean like him?" Peter asked, nodding towards her sleeping brother.

LooAnne nodded, "I know that the Lord can save us from Will and Cliff but then what's to happen after that? If we get out of here what will I tell him? Part of me wants to just let us both go our different ways but I wonder if I can even do that knowing that he's my twin brother."

"Why wouldn't you wanna tell him?" Peter questioned.

"I don't know," LooAnne admitted. "I guess I always assumed that he would grow up like our older brothers, that he would be a threat to me. When I ran away seven years ago I wanted to leave all this behind. I never imagined I would get so caught up in it again. I just can't seem to lose the past."

Peter only nodded, keeping quiet as LooAnne went on. "This is all my fault, you know," she whispered. "Had I never left here none of us would be in this situation. You would be home with your family, Clara wouldn't be heartbroken, Uncle Ricky wouldn't be worried sick as I know he is, Uncle Robert wouldn't have to worry about pretending I'm his child when he hates me. So many things would be right if I hadn't run away."

"And you and your brothers?" Peter asked.

LooAnne looked up at the deputy thoughtfully. "I don't know," she admitted. "The possibilities are endless. I really don't know where we would be."

"You did what any other kid in your situation would have done," Peter said.

LooAnne shook her head in disagreement. "Had the Lord intended me for this life I took, He would have put me there, as it is I tried to run away and take it only to end up back here where He did put me."

Peter shook his head, "Not necessarily. It doesn't matter where you start out, the Almighty can use you from wherever you are no matter what. What matters is where you end up and the path you took to get there. He started you out the daughter of a killer and then guided you to who you are now, the niece and heiress o' one o' the richest men in the country. I don't know what His plan is but I do know that there ain't no stoppin' it. Everything that's happened, whether it be over the last seven years or the last seven hours, is a part of His plan and the good thing about it is, His plan is perfect."

LooAnne smiled even though Peter could not see it in the dark, "Thank you, Deputy. You're very right."

"So were you when you left this place, Miss Nash," Peter assured. "Nothin' o' what's happened these past few days has been your fault. And now you get to be the one to help stop it. Maybe that was His plan all along?"

LooAnne looked out the window thoughtfully, mulling over every word Peter had spoken. Never before had she heard that many words come from the reticent deputy, and when they had they were full of knowledge and understanding which only caused her to fall harder for him.

She only hoped that come morning his plan would work...

After her short conversation with Peter, LooAnne had finally managed to doze off a bit. Seated just under the window where the night breeze cooled her, she had rested as comfortably as possible until rudely awakened by the sound of angry footsteps bounding up the stairs!

The dawn was just breaking, a small trickle of light

peeking through the trees and into the broken window, a rude contrast to the tense situation the three prisoners soon found themselves in.

Stephen was just able to get out of the way of the door before it was flung open by a vengeful Will Luther! Determination etched on his face, Will took less than a glance around the room before his eyes locked on LooAnne who stood in the corner by the window! He wasted no time in crossing the room and seizing her arm angrily!

Stephen stood back, looking on in shock while Peter recovered nicely from his rude awakening and leaped to his feet. He was about to lunge at Will when an unfamiliar voice from the doorway stopped him!

"Hold still, Deputy!" Ray Luther was positioned just inside the room with a shotgun in his hands, ready to end any confrontation they might have with Peter and Stephen. Will took hold of LooAnne and started to roughly drag her from the room as she struggled to get away from him! Though she tried every trick she knew he pinned her arms behind her back, forcing her to comply as he made his way towards the door!

Peter was torn between his desire to stay alive and the need to help LooAnne who would soon be beyond his assistance if they made it out the door! This had not been how they had planned their escape but Peter knew they would have to take this chance or risk never having another!

LooAnne had been thinking the same thing and decided to take action praying that Peter and Stephen would act accordingly. She fought as hard as she could and then, without warning, slumped over in a faint directly on top of

Ray's shotgun barrel! LooAnne had barely made it to the floor when Peter lunged for Will, tackling him to the ground in the hallway as Stephen made a go for Ray! LooAnne instantly leaped up and made a grab for the fallen shotgun only to have Ray take hold of her and throw her to the side as he tried to shake off Stephen and grab the firearm!

Stephen fought hard against Ray but was unable to block a blow to the jaw that sent him stumbling backward down the stairs! As his cousin crashed to the bottom Ray dove for his shotgun and had just put his hands on it when LooAnne grabbed a loose post from the top of the banister and struck him over the head as hard as she could! Ray dropped to the ground in unconsciousness as the post broke over his head! Peter and Will were both still going strong, throwing each other to one side and then the next, each giving and receiving blows. LooAnne ran to the bottom of the stairs where Stephen lay dazed, his arm bent loosely to the side.

The moment LooAnne touched it he cried out in pain and she knew it was broken!

"We've got to get you to a doctor," she thought aloud. "Can you stand?"

Stephen, his face creased with pain, nodded feebly and leaned on LooAnne as she helped him up.

She turned to look at the top of the stairs where Peter had just delivered a punch to Will's jaw.

"Go!" he yelled as Will came at him again.

LooAnne could not bring herself to leave Peter to face her brother alone, especially when she had been the reason for the situation they now found themselves in. She had to help him somehow but was at a loss as to what she could do. LooAnne's mind was still whirling when Peter yelled, "LooAnne! Get out! Don't Stop!"

LooAnne was unsure if it was the command in his voice or the way her name sounded when he spoke it but she knew she had no choice but to do as he said. Taking one last look as Will drove his fist into the young deputy's stomach, LooAnne turned and hurried as fast as Stephen could move out the front door, praying that somehow Peter would get out!

LooAnne helped her twin down the porch steps, all the while looking around frantically for some kind of vehicle to aid their escape, but she saw none. Seeing no other alternative LooAnne turned towards the woods and ran, Stephen lagging behind, pain pulsing through his core with every anxious step. The two ran as fast as they could until the house was out of sight. LooAnne looked back over her shoulder every second praying she would see Peter run from the house, but she never did. A small haze shone through the trees, lighting the dew on the underbrush. LooAnne and Stephen plowed forward through the bramble, both of them desperate to get away from the Luther's. LooAnne looked back once more before the Luther Estate disappeared, hoping beyond hope that she would see Peter, but he never appeared and soon she and her brother were running down the hill out of sight of the Luther house.

Please, Lord, please get him out! She prayed, her heart sinking as she realized she may never see the young deputy alive again!

TWELVE

Heart and Soul

LooAnne and Stephen bounded down the steep hill away from the Luther Estate. Both running as quickly as they could without slipping on the damp ground. LooAnne was quite a bit in front of her brother and when she no longer heard his footsteps behind her she stopped and turned only to find him leaning heavily against a tree. His face was red and dripping with sweat, his broken arm hanging loosely at his side as he struggled to ketch his breath.

LooAnne was next to him in an instant, her heart beating wildly as she went to examine his arm.

"No," Stephen shook his head in protest, "Keep goin', there ain't no way I can make it."

"I'm not leaving you here," LooAnne informed him.

"Th-they'll come after us," Stephen panted, "Ya got to."

LooAnne only shook her head, having no intention of leaving her brother again. Whether he knew it or not she could not help the feeling of responsibility towards him. He had depended on her only to have her abandon him at the first chance of freedom and she determined in her mind that she would never make that mistake again.

"They're gonna come after us, you gotta go!" Stephen demanded, wincing with every word as he clutched his arm.

"I will not leave you here," LooAnne said sternly. "Peter can take Will; I know he can!"

"No you don't! He's no match for a Luther. Once Will's taken care o' the deputy he'll come after us and if you're not outta here he'll take us both back and you know where that'll lead!"

"He will *not* take us back! I'll die before I go back to that place. Now we've got to find somewhere safe to wait for Peter."

"What if he doesn't come?" Stephen spoke the reality that LooAnne was trying hard not to dwell on.

She swallowed hard, Peter's words echoing in her mind, *"Don't stop!"*. "You're right," she sighed, "We can't stop. We can't take the chance that Will or Ray will come instead."

"Just go, get out of here before they come! I'll never be able to keep up with you."

"No, you can do it, you have to," LooAnne was still determined not to leave Stephen. The possibility that she had already lost Peter was nearly too much for her to bear, she knew she could not stand to lose her brother as well. "We'll take it slower, you can make it."

"Make it to where?" Stephen asked looking around him at the trees. "Town is miles from here." Then he narrowed his eyes suspiciously at LooAnne, "Wait, I know what you're thinking. No! I'll not go to the Nash Estate!"

"Why?" LooAnne asked, flabbergasted.

"Miss Nash, in case you've forgotten I'm a Luther. The Nash's – *you* – are my mother's family, a family that she hurt and betrayed when she ran away. I can't show my face in front of them!"

If only you knew. LooAnne though. *If only you knew she was my mother too.*

"That's ridiculous!" LooAnne protested, withholding her inward emotions at mention of their connected family.

"You're a member of the Nash family just as much as I am. You might be a Luther but you've done nothing wrong and you need help!"

"It don't matter what I want. I don't belong there any more than my father would. You're a Nash, you should know that!"

"I do know that," LooAnne informed Stephen firmly. "I know that more than you will ever understand. I know that things are not well between our two families and I know why, but that does not mean I'm going to leave you out here to be killed by your brother and cousin."

"Why? Why can't you leave me out here? I'm nothing to you, Miss Nash. I nearly got you killed!"

LooAnne sighed, knowing she could not explain her feelings to Stephen without telling him who she was.

"Stephen, please, just trust me. I promise you will be more than welcome at the Nash Estate. But we can't stand here and argue any longer when they could be after us as we speak! The estates only three miles away it's closer than town, you'll be able to make it much faster."

"They'll know that's the first place we would go!" Stephen continued to protest.

"And if we can get there before they catch up to us we'll be protected. Now please come?"

Stephen looked at the sunrise through the trees, looking pained and defeated. "Fine," he sighed. "But if they ketch up to us you gotta promise to run on and leave me if I can't keep up!"

LooAnne nodded, "I promise."

The two turned and started making their way up the hill to their left, going as fast as Stephen's arm would allow. He looked beyond pained but tried his best not to let it slow his pace, knowing it could mean their lives. LooAnne could not take her mind from Peter Andrews. Her heart yearned to know what had become of him, if he had escaped and was running through the woods or been beaten in the fight and was now locked in the bedroom completely at Will's mercy, of which he would have none. LooAnne longed to turn back and find Peter but his words played over and over in her mind telling her not to stop, so she didn't. She could not overcome the thought of him being harmed because of her, and by her own brother. LooAnne knew that it would not be easy to fight an enraged, power hungry Luther, but if anyone could do it Peter Andrews could. And that was the thought that kept her going, knowing that the Lord would be with him.

As the dawn slowly turned to day the sun grew hot as it ascended into the sky. LooAnne and Stephen had made good time for only a short while before the latter began to weaken from the pain in his broken arm. He stumbled along behind LooAnne, his face pale and eyes blood-shot. His wavy red hair matted to his forehead with sweat that drenched him.

LooAnne's throat was parched and her stomach growled for food which she had not had since being taken from Belle Hall. Her head was aching from where Will had struck her, causing her great fatigue as they made their way towards the Nash Estate.

LooAnne glanced back at Stephen and realized how badly he needed rest but she also knew that they were only a matter of yards from her uncle's land. She determined that once they had crossed they could rest by the river in the valley before heading the rest of the way to the estate.

In silence they walked on, both in pain and fatigued but thankful that somehow Will and Ray were not pursuing them...at least not to their knowledge. Both knew very well that their brother and cousin could appear at any moment and take them prisoner again, or worse!

LooAnne's mind had been dwelling solely on Peter from the moment they had left him fighting for their freedom at the Luther Estate. She knew that his chances of beating a skilled fighter such as her brother were slim but she held on to the knowledge that the Lord would be with him.

She kept her eyes ahead of her, knowing that the fence separating the Luther's land from the Nash's was not far. She had come this way many times before, the most memorable being the day she had come to the fence and crossed it with no intention of turning back.

Only by the Lord's grace and her uncle's fear of the Luther's widespread knowledge had they not found her in previous years. She had been so close, only a few miles away from her father's family and yet her location had remained unknown to them due to Ricky's protection during the first few years of her life with him until she had so much matured that chances of her being recognized her slim.

She could hear Stephen moving along slowly behind her and could only imagine the hardship he endured with every step that wracked his pained body. If they could only reach the fence LooAnne knew they would be able to rest with less chance of being caught by her relatives. Finally, after nearly two hours of walking in the heat, LooAnne spotted the sunlight reflecting off the shining metal of her uncle's fence line!

"There's the fence!" she exclaimed, hurrying her pace towards it with Stephen close behind. She ran toward the barbed wire strung through the midst of the woods, nearly overtaken with bramble but encasing the only place in the world where LooAnne felt she could not be touched by the Luther's!

The moment she reached it she lifted the loose middle wire and slipped under, helping her brother who followed slowly, wincing as he squeezed between the barbs.

"We made it," LooAnne sighed with relief, brushing a bit of sweaty hair to the side. "Come on, I know where we can rest for a little while and get some water."

Stephen nodded, his eyes scanning the open fields before him, cut in half by the rushing waters of a creek that fed the ponds and water holes of the Nash Estate.

"How much farther to the house?" he asked, his voice cracking from lack of hydration.

"It's just over that hill," LooAnne pointed. "Behind those trees."

Stephen nodded and followed LooAnne through the tall, swaying grass towards the creek where they found a shady spot to stop and drink. Stephen dropped to his knees next to the water and used his good hand to scoop some into his mouth thirstily. LooAnne did likewise, sighing with relief as the cool liquid coated her throat and stomach.

Stephen splashed his sweaty face, wetting his curly red hair before laying back on the dirt and closing his eyes in exhaustion. LooAnne sat back and looked at him, gazing at her brother thoughtfully, realizing for the first time since they met how much he resembled their father. Had it not been for his mother's red hair and light brown eyes LooAnne realized that he could be the exact image of his father; broad yet lanky and strong with a light complexion darkened a bit by the sun.

As she stared at him the faded memory of her father was renewed in her mind and she wondered what things would have been like had he and Amanda not been killed. *I may never have left,* she thought to herself. *I might still be a Luther.* But she knew that no matter how she wondered what life would be like if her parents were still alive there was no way to know for sure, no way to go back and change it all, and LooAnne wondered if given the opportunity she even would.

Stephen opened his eyes and caught his sister staring at him, for a moment a hint of recognition flashed through his mind, as though he knew this young Nash from a lifetime before, but soon it was gone. He knew that it was to be expected for her to resemble the family from which his mother had been born. LooAnne was, after all, his cousin, or so he thought, and there was no question that she bore the Nash features as he and his brothers did. *And Beth,* he thought silently, memories of his sister entering his mind as they so often did. Though they had spent every day until their youth together he remembered her vaguely, having tried to put her out of his mind the moment he learned she had disappeared. She had left him without a word, only a silent goodbye as he drifted off to sleep that night with her face staring over him, a strange glow about it, a glow of freedom and determination. *If only I had known then what she planned to do,* he thought. But it was too late to mourn the loss of his only sister. Whether she was dead or not, to him she was gone forever.

"How's your arm?" LooAnne's voice broke Stephen from the thoughts of his sister and back to the unrelenting pain of his broken arm.

"Numb," he answered honestly.

"You can't feel it?" LooAnne asked hopefully.

Stephen shook his head, "Not that numb I'm afraid."

LooAnne sighed and nodded, "We'll be at the estate soon and get you to a doctor."

"If your uncle doesn't have me shot the minute he sees me."

"Uncle Ricky would never do such a thing," LooAnne defended.

"Why not?" Stephen asked bitterly. "I'm a Luther, the worthless offspring of his rebellious sister."

"Despite what others may think Uncle Ricky loved his sister no matter what she did."

"I suppose he loved her for running away and causing their father to die of shock and worry and then giving the Luther's four children to raise as killers? Excuse me, Miss Nash, but even your uncle ain't a saint."

LooAnne huffed, "My uncle loved his sister no matter what she did, she made a mistake and paid dearly for it. He's long since forgiven her for the heartbreak she caused, though he was angry he never stopped loving her."

Stephen shook his head, "Don't mean he's gonna love me. I might be his sister's son but I'm just as much a Luther as my father was."

LooAnne shook her head, "It doesn't matter what your father was, it matters what you are. The things your family did in the past do not have to dictate who you are in the present and future. You've got the Luther's blood no matter what you do, but you have your own heart and soul and it's up to you what you do with them. My uncle isn't going to judge you for who your father was but for who *you* are here and now."

Stephen stared at LooAnne for a moment, wrapping his mind around the words she had just spoken. Was she right? Did he really have the power to get away from what he was born into just by changing the desires of his heart? He had never taken a liking to the things his family had forced him to do, but he had thought since childhood that he was doomed to the life of a Luther, knowing he was forever tainted by their name.

"Even if your uncle won't hate me there are lots o' people who will," he said. "I can never have a normal life. No one would ever want to have anything to do with me."

"But isn't that what you were doing when you escaped your brother and got the job at the mill, starting a new life?" LooAnne asked. "You changed your name, you were working, and you were living the life of a righteous man safely away from the influence and pressure of your family. You can do that again."

"No I can't!" Stephen insisted. "I tried and you see how it worked. I ended up right back where I started."

"So instead of trying again you're going to give up and throw away your life to live like a criminal because your father was one?"

"I don't have a choice! You think I haven't done things against the law? You think there ain't some warrant out fer me somewhere? I was raised a Luther; I was forced to do things that can get me thrown in jail!"

"Exactly! You were *forced* to do those things! Did you want to? Was it your choice?"

Stephen shook his head vigorously, "Of course not! I didn't want to steal and fight any more than I wanted to kidnap you but did I do it? Yes, yes I did. I'm a thief and a kidnapper."

"I don't know why you were forced to steal but I do know that you kidnapped me to protect Clara Andrews, you were forced to by your brothers who have bullied you all your life. You can't be held accountable for what they made you do," LooAnne stated.

"But it's too late now!" Stephen insisted, his voice rising. "It's too late for me! I can't have a normal life, I tried and it didn't work. My life will always ketch up with me. You're better off leaving me here to be killed by my brother."

"Your brother made his choices just as you have to make yours, just as I had to make mine! We all have to choose what we're going to do with our lives and it's up to us whether or not we live them the way God intended or the devilish ways of the world! Now, Luther or not you're hurt and in need of a doctor so you're coming to the estate with me whether you want to or not. After that you can go your way and I'll go mine. But I hope that you'll see things my way and forget that you're a Luther and live the life of a respectable man."

LooAnne was surprised by the words that flowed fluently from her mouth. How could she tell Stephen to forget his past when she herself could not? How could she expect him to move on with a life she herself had dwelled in for years? LooAnne knew exactly how her brother was feeling, she had once thought the same things he now did,

150

that it was hopeless for her because of who she had been born to. And now she realized that Stephen was not the only one who needed to take her advice; maybe she needed some of it too.

Stephen looked at the ground and sighed in dejection, "I wish I could live a respectable life," he said earnestly, "but my past will always catch up with me. It's already prevented me from having the one thing I want."

"You mean Clara," LooAnne thought aloud.

Stephen nodded sadly. "She must hate me."

LooAnne knelt next to her brother and looked him in the eye, "Stephen, she doesn't hate you. I talked to her the day after you were supposed to meet her and she was hurt and afraid for you but she loves you just as much as you love her."

Stephen Parker looked up from the ground to stare into LooAnne's eyes, searching for any hint of a lie but he found none.

"How can she still love me after I left her like that?"

"You didn't leave her, Stephen, you were taken. She's afraid for you, she's been afraid for you since you told her you were in danger. If you come back to the estate with me you can call her and explain, you can tell her everything."

For a moment Stephen's hopes were rising, maybe once he told her the truth he could court her with her father's permission and profess his love for her without secrecy? But then his hopes were dashed with one thought. Her brother...

Stephen shook his head and stood up, trying to ignore the throbbing pain in his arm. "I can't," he said, exasperated.

"Why?" LooAnne asked, also rising.

"Because if it weren't for me her brother would be alive

and well right now."

"We've got no reason to believe he's not," LooAnne said, feeling her throat beginning to squeeze.

"We've got every reason to believe he's not. He was fighting with Will Luther, there's no way he made it outta there. He might not be dead but he sure ain't in a good way and it's my fault. Clara will want nothin' to do with me, Miss Nash."

LooAnne couldn't find the right words to speak, her own heart aching at her brother's words. Was it too much to hope that Peter was alive and had gotten away? Maybe Stephen had been right? Maybe there was no escape from the terrors of a Luther's life?

"I'm sorry," LooAnne's brother spoke apologetically, seeing LooAnne's faltering expression.

She just shook her head, deciding that the quicker they got to the Nash Estate the quicker they could get help to Peter. "We've got to get moving. The Luther's could be out here anywhere."

Stephen nodded without a word and together they left the protective shade of the creek and ventured across the grassland towards the house.

The sun was high above the mountain before the grounds of the Nash Estate finally came into view. The main house stood tall and bold against the surrounding fields and road, it's dark brown walls blending well with the open prairie, lined with fences and gates. Once a prosperous plantation, the stables and bunkhouse stood to the west surrounded by tangled lines of fencing and corrals. The fields beyond were lined with grain, corn, and tobacco; horses and cattle grazing on the surrounding hills.

LooAnne was so enlightened by the sight that she instantly

took off running, the thought of seeing her uncle and being held in his tight embrace spurring her on. She ran through an open gate and up the hill before calling, "Uncle Ricky!" Moments later the back door was thrown open and two men appeared, one being a guard whom her uncle had on duty, the other being her uncle's steward and best friend, Chris Block. LooAnne knew him well, one of the only men on earth that her uncle trusted with his possessions and his life. Chris had been present when LooAnne had first arrived at the Nash Estate as a child and was among the very few who knew her secret.

"Miss Nash!" he cried, the relief on his lined face evident as he ran down the steps of the back porch to meet her. They embraced for only a moment before LooAnne asked, "Where's Uncle Ricky?" her chest heaved as she attempted to catch her breath, holding onto Chris' arms for support as he examined her disheveled appearance.

"He's still not returned from his business trip," the stewards said. "I sent for him the moment we heard of your disappearance but he's not due for another few hours. Oh, Miss Nash, you had us all worried sick! Are you alright?"

LooAnne swallowed hard and nodded, "We managed to escape," she explained. "But we must send someone to help the Dallas deputy. We don't think he got out!"

"We?" Chris asked as his eyes landed on Stephen Parker who was just reaching them.

LooAnne turned to Stephen and said, "Mr. Block this is Stephen Parker, he was taken prisoner as well. Stephen this is my uncle's steward, Chris Block."

Stephen nodded the greeting as did Chris, though the latter looked at the young man suspiciously he said nothing to question him.

"Mr. Block, we think Stephen's broken his arm, he needs a doctor as soon as possible."

Chris nodded and said, "Come, we'll get you both fixed up and call the doctor. Do you know who it was that took you?"

LooAnne looked around to make certain none of the staff were listening before she turned warning eyes on her uncle's steward. "It was the Luther's, Mr. Block," she whispered causing Chris' eyes to widen as they darted from LooAnne's face to Stephen's and then back again. Knowing that she was not at liberty to speak in front of the stranger, Chris nodded stiffly and led the way inside the beautiful house, all the while wondering what horrors LooAnne would have to tell him.

THIRTEEN

My Brother

Chris wasted no time in getting one of the maids to summon a doctor from town. He was anxious to learn whether or not the Luther's knew of LooAnne's secret but knew he could not ask until they were alone. That moment soon came when Stephen was taken to one of the vacant bedrooms to get cleaned up, leaving LooAnne and Chris alone in the downstairs hall.

"I'll send the doctor up as soon as he arrives," Chris promised Stephen as he and the butler ascended the stairs. Once they were out of sight the steward turned worried eyes on his employer's niece. "What happened?" he asked anxiously, "Do they know?"

LooAnne sighed and shook her head, "No, they think only that I'm LooAnne Nash and nothing more."

"Why did they take you then?"

"Revenge," LooAnne stated plainly. "They want Uncle Ricky and I to pay for what happened in town last summer."

"I see," Chris sighed in displeasure and ran a nervous hand through his graying hair. "Well, you're safe here until Mr. Nash arrives," he assured LooAnne. "You must be exhausted, Miss Nash. Go up to your room and I'll send one of the maids with some food and the doctor can look at that cut on your forehead."

"It's fine, Mr. Block, I -"

"I insist, Miss Nash," Chris said firmly and LooAnne relented, not having the energy to argue. Turning, she climbed the staircase to the second floor and opened the door to her large bedroom. Though not as grand as the one at Belle Hall, LooAnne's bedroom was well furnished with a high posted bed, bureau, dresser, and daybed. The warm color of the walls and thick carpet beneath her feet, mixed with the familiar smell of home caused LooAnne's nerves to relax a bit as she paused in the middle of her room, absorbing the moment of calmness. She breathed a sigh of relief and closed her eyes, imagining she were a little girl just getting home form her tutorial, forgetting, if only for a few seconds, the turmoil which her past life had brought back. But this lasted for only a moment before there was a knock at the door.

"Come in," LooAnne called.

One of the house maids, whom LooAnne knew very well, entered the room carrying a small tray with a glass of water.

"Are you alright, ma-am?" she asked with concern.

LooAnne nodded, "Just in need of a bath and some clean clothes."

The middle-aged woman nodded vigorously. "I'll start the bath right away, Miss Nash."

LooAnne thanked her and then pulled open the doors of the long closets where she was faced with lines of clothes she had decided not to take to Dallas. Among them LooAnne found something comfortable to change into and then proceeded to remove her torn and soiled attire. As she did she could not help but catch sight of herself in the mirror atop the bureau. She noticed just how unsightly she looked. Her bobbed hair was in disarray and her blouse and skirt both torn and muddy. Blood from where Will had hit her stained her collar and she could now see the severity of the wound. It ran just above her eyebrow and was matted with dried blood and dirt from where her head had struck the rock.

LooAnne enjoyed her hot bath all the while anticipating the arrival of her uncle at any moment. She longed to see him, to tell him of all that had happened in the short while since she had left the Nash Estate. LooAnne knew that he would not be happy to learn of her encounter with the Luther's or that he indeed was housing one to whom she was so closely related, but nevertheless, she yearned to tell him, knowing that he would help her.

After she was cleaned up and changed into a complete garb of stockings, skirt, crepe blouse, and boots LooAnne was seen by the doctor who put a bandage on her head and told her to rest as much as possible for the next few days. He said that Stephen's arm was indeed broken and that he had put it in a splint and sling for the next few months. LooAnne thanked him for coming so quickly and just as he was leaving an officer from town arrived. LooAnne met with him in her uncle's study and related the entire incident to him in full, leaving out the very significant fact that she herself was a Luther.

"So Andrews is still up there then?" the officer asked. LooAnne nodded, "As far as we know he is. He was fighting with one of the Luther's to give us the chance to escape and we never saw him after that."

The lawman nodded and jotted down what LooAnne had said on his note pad.

"And you say the Luther's kidnapped you because you and Mr. Nash were involved in the apprehension of their family last year?"

LooAnne nodded wearily, "That's what he said."

The officer nodded and rose from his seat, extending his hand to LooAnne who shook it. "Thank you, Miss Nash. I'm very sorry for all of this. You can be sure we'll send someone to the Luther Estate to get Peter Andrews and those Luther's will never bother you again."

If only that were true, LooAnne thought though she smiled gratefully at the officer. "Thank you, sir. Would you please let me know if you find Deputy Andrews?"

The middle-aged lawman nodded. "Of course. There's no guarantee they'll still be at the Luther place but if they are we'll get 'em."

LooAnne smiled wanly and nodded, her worry for Peter growing as the minutes passed.

"I'll need to talk with Stephen Parker as well," the officer added.

"He's upstairs resting," LooAnne said. "Would it be possible to wait until this afternoon?"

She had not told the officer Stephen's true identity as he had not given her leave to and decided that she wanted her uncle's advice before revealing anything related to her twin brother. The officer was reluctant but anxious to get a search started for his fellow lawman and agreed to speaking with Stephen that afternoon once he had rested. Again he expressed his apologies for what had happened and Chris showed him out, leaving LooAnne alone in her uncle's study.

She stared after the two men, looking into nothingness as her mind raced with worries. She could only imagine the terrible things her brother and cousin could do to Peter, the horrors he would be forced to endure for allowing her and Stephen to escape. That was if he was even still alive! Images of her brother killing him swept through LooAnne's mind and she shook her head vigorously trying to wipe them away. *He'll be alright,* she told herself though she knew that was very unlikely.

A knot began to grow in LooAnne's throat as she dropped down on the sofa and buried her face in her hands, trying to withhold the moisture behind her eyes. This was no time to cry over something she could no longer help and yet the thought that she might have prevented it weighed heavily on her heart.

Had it not been for me he wouldn't be there now, she thought. *I never should have left here.*

"LooAnne?" The deep, familiar voice was filled with concern and anxiety but it instantly caused LooAnne's heart to leap! She looked up and in an instant was in her uncle's arms, holding onto him tightly as he hugged her!

"Oh, Uncle Ricky!" she whispered, feeling her nerves come to an instant calm.

Her uncle held her tightly, relief flooding his lined face. "LooAnne Marie Nash, you scared me to death," he scolded before pulling away to examine his niece for injury. "Are you alright? What happened to your head?" LooAnne shook her head, "It's nothing I promise, just a little -"

"Little nothing, that bandage is huge. LooAnne, what happened? Who was it?"

Ricky's eyes were filled with worry and confusion as he

held LooAnne at arm's length waiting for her to answer his questions.

"It-it was the Luther's," LooAnne whispered, feeling all her bottled up emotions threatening to spill.

Ricky's eyes widened, his grip tightening on her shoulders. "The Luther's!" he exclaimed. "Did they hurt you? Do they know?"

LooAnne shook her head, "Besides the forehead, no they didn't hurt me and I don't think they know who I am. They said they wanted revenge on you and I for getting all those Luther's killed and jailed, nothing about me being their sister."

"You were taken by your brothers!" Ricky exclaimed before looking about him to ensure no one had heard.

LooAnne swallowed hard and nodded. "Cliff is still in jail in Dallas but Will and our cousin Ray decided to carry out the plan of revenge without him."

Ricky pulled LooAnne into another hug as a tear escaped her eye and ran down her cheek.

"It's alright," he whispered reassuringly. "They can't do anything to you here. How did you get away?"

LooAnne sniffled a bit and pulled away from her uncle, drying her eyes as she began to explain. "I wasn't the only one they took; Mr. and Mrs. Andrews' son was with me. They used him to get me to go with them without a fight."

"Where is he?" Ricky asked, sensing the fear in his niece's voice.

"He didn't make it out," LooAnne whispered, choking on her words. "He tackled Will and was fighting him, he told me to take Stephen and run and I did. We never saw him again after that."

"Who's Stephen?" Ricky asked, looking extremely

confused.

LooAnne rubbed her hands together as she walked across the room, wondering how she was going to tell her uncle about Stephen Parker. How she would explain that she had her twin brother upstairs and that he wasn't like the rest of her family as she had imagined.

"LooAnne," Ricky probed. "Who is Stephen?"

LooAnne sighed and turned back to face her uncle. "He was caught with Peter and I," she started. "They forced him to come into Belle Hall and take me. He tried to argue with them but they threatened to hurt the girl he's in love with and he had no choice."

Ricky frowned, knowing that LooAnne was concealing something from him, "Where is he now?" he asked.

"Upstairs," LooAnne stated plainly. "He broke his arm when we escaped and the doctor told him to rest after he had something on his stomach. Mr. Block is taking care of him."

"I see," Ricky searched his niece's eyes, wondering what was causing her to look so conflicted. "There's more isn't there?" he asked.

LooAnne looked down and nodded.

"What is it?"

"He..." LooAnne trailed off, too nervous to finish.

"He what, LooAnne?" Ricky persisted.

"He-he's....my brother." The words escaped her mouth with such little volume that Ricky barely heard her but when he did his eyes grew wide and his face flushed with anger.

"LooAnne, what are you saying?" he demanded, his voice full of tension.

"My twin brother is upstairs. He wants to start a new life,

he's tired of being pushed around and hurt by Will and Cliff."

"So you brought him *here*?"

LooAnne nodded firmly, not once questioning her decision. "Yes I did, Uncle Ricky. He's not like Will and Cliff, he wants to make an honest living and have a family. He tried to start over with a new name and a new job but our brothers found him and forced him to help them take me. He's had a bad life and has been put through a lot of hardship. When we were little he was my responsibility and I did everything I could to protect him from our family until I left. I abandoned him once, I can't do it again!"

Ricky looked at LooAnne for a moment, his mind taking in every word she had said before his angered expression faded.

"I'm sorry, my dear," he apologized. "It's not because he's a Luther, it's just hard on an old man to imagine seeing the son of his sister for the first time. Knowing he's up there, that he's Amanda's boy and your brother," Ricky shook his head, "it strikes me strangely."

LooAnne nodded, "It did me too."

"Does he know about you?"

LooAnne shook her head, "No, I couldn't bring myself to tell him. I'm afraid that he harbors an inward hate for Beth Luther and as long as I'm LooAnne Nash he'll think well of me. Right or not, I don't want him to hate me."

"Why would he hate you?"

"I left him, Uncle Ricky. I was all he had in the world and I left him with the thought that his turning out like our father and brothers was inevitable. I never gave him a chance to have a different life until today. Why shouldn't he hate me?"

"You're his sister, LooAnne. He may have been bitter for a time but you'll never know if you don't confront him with the truth."

"I'd rather he never know the truth than have it be that he dislikes me."

Ricky laid a hand on his niece's shoulder, looking her in the eye, "It's your decision to make, my dear, but all this happened for a reason. You two were thrown into each other's path after seven years of thinking you would never see the other again. Wouldn't it be worth the risk to have your brother back?"

LooAnne thought for a moment, wondering if she even wanted him back. Her life as LooAnne Nash had been a dream come true and all her brothers had done was hurt it. Now that she was faced with the decision she didn't know what to do.

"And also," Ricky added, "if you do decide to tell him you must be certain he's trustworthy. Otherwise he might spread the word around. You don't know him all that well. It might be wise to wait until you do."

LooAnne nodded in agreement. "Or maybe not tell him at all."

Ricky shrugged his shoulders a bit. "It's your decision to make, LooAnne."

His niece nodded, her mind wandering once more to Peter Andrews.

"I'm going to get some rest," she told her uncle wearily, hoping that when she woke there would be news of his recovery. "If the police call about Peter come and wake me."

Her uncle nodded, the wheels in his mind turning as he watched his niece climb the stairs, wondering if there was something going on between she and the Dallas deputy.

FOURTEEN

Nightmare

The noon passed peacefully with both LooAnne and Stephen resting comfortably in their bedrooms. Ricky sat alone in the study below, his mind wandering off in one direction and then the next. Should the authorities fail to apprehend Will and Ray Luther it would mean a great deal of confinement for both LooAnne and her brother. His mind was also engaged with the thoughts of his new found nephew who he had yet to meet. Wondering what, as the young man's uncle, his duties were towards him. He knew he would be obliged to offer Stephen a job at the estate or one of his other business but if he did so would it not put his niece in a very precarious position to be so close to her brother who was ignorant of their relationship? But if their older brother and cousin were not captured and continued to pose a threat to both LooAnne and her uncle, Ricky decided that it would be safest to leave the state where Will and Ray would hopefully be contained until they were put behind bars for good.

Ricky was deep in contemplation when there was a knock on the open study door. Ricky looked up just as Chris entered and said, "Excuse me, sir, but the Sheriff is out here wanting to talk to Miss Nash."

Ricky rose from his seat and said, "Send him in here. I don't want to wake her if he doesn't have any news."

Chris nodded and disappeared for a few moments before showing Sheriff Murphy into the study.

The officer was perspiring heavily and looked quite elated. Ricky shook his hand and asked, "I hope you have good news for me, Matt."

The sheriff nodded vigorously, "I do, Mr. Nash. We went to the Luther place and found a vehicle outside so we broke in. Will Luther wasn't there but we got Ray."

"Will got away?" Ricky asked, feeling his heart beginning to sink.

Murphy nodded, "We waited for him but he never showed. One of the men is back at the office tryin' to break Ray of some information but so far he won't say a thing."

"And Deputy Andrews?"

Sheriff Murphy's face fell and he shook his head, "Not a sign of him. We suspect Will took him somewhere but we don't know where or why. We've got men combing the entire county for 'em."

Ricky nodded, "What do you think his chances are?"

Murphy shook his head, "If the Luther's are as bad now as they've proved themselves to be over the years.... I just hope we get to Andrews before they're through with him."

Ricky nodded, "So do I. Mr. and Mrs. Andrews are fine people, I hate to think that my nephews may be responsible for the loss of their son."

"So do I, Mr. Nash, but we'll do all we can I promise you that."

"I know you will, Matt. Keep me posted."

Sheriff Murphy nodded, said his farewells, and left.

Moments later LooAnne came bounding down the stairs, having seen the sheriff leave and anxious to hear news on the young deputy.

"Uncle Ricky, did they find him?" she asked, pausing half way down the stairs.

Ricky shook his head solemnly. "I'm afraid not, my dear. They did catch Ray but Sheriff Murphy said Will had taken Peter out of the house."

Upon hearing this LooAnne' heart sank and the color drained from her face. "He wouldn't do that unless..."

"LooAnne, don't jump to conclusions," Ricky tried to reassure her but it had little effect.

"This is all my fault," LooAnne exclaimed. "Peter's been killed and it's all because of me!" Turning in anguish LooAnne ran down the remaining steps and out the back entrance, her uncle calling after her but unable to stop her as she ran to the stables in tears.

LooAnne threw open the stable door and then slammed it closed behind her, glad to find that the long isle of stalls was vacant of ranch hands. Tears were already falling down her face, wetting her chin and neck. LooAnne leaned against the stable wall, closing her eyes against the pain and guilt which bubbled up from within her. Her brother must have killed Peter, there was no other explanation as to why he would take him from the house and leave Ray behind. LooAnne could still picture the young deputy fighting valiantly, allowing herself and Stephen to escape, knowing that his chances were slim.

LooAnne remembered the day Peter had told her he did not hold her past against her, she remembered the new feeling of total acceptance she had felt when hearing him, knowing that there was someone in the world besides her uncle who did not condemn her for what her past had been. And now she realized it had been that very thing that had gotten him killed.

LooAnne buried her face in her hands and cried, the thought of Peter dying, being killed by the hands of the Luther's, becoming too much for her to bear.

She sobbed bitterly, overwhelmed with emotions of mixed anger, regret, and sorrow. LooAnne was about to drop to the stable floor when a venomous voice cut through her cries!

"Well isn't this convenient!"

LooAnne's head instantly snapped up and the sight that met her eyes filled her with both joy and fear. There, standing at the other end of the stable hallway gun in hand, was Will Luther! And with him, beaten and bruised but standing tall, was Peter Andrews! His hands were bound behind his back and Will had the barrel of a pistol trained on his temple, but he was alive, and to LooAnne, it was the greatest sight she had laid eyes on since the day's beginning.

"Peter," she whispered.

Will laughed as if amused by the situation. "You seem outta sorts, Miss Nash," he mocked as a smirk found its way on his face. "Or should I say, Miss Luther?"

LooAnne's overjoyed heart immediately sank and she paled, taking a step back from her brother.

"W-what are you talk-"

"Oh don't play dumb with me, Beth. I know who ya are."

LooAnne shook her head, fear overtaking every inch of her body as she was faced with her worst nightmare.

"How?" she croaked, an unwelcome feeling of defeat coming over her.

Will snorted, "I gotta admit it took me a while but I finally figured it out. After you disappeared seven years ago we looked everywhere for ya but it was like you'd dropped off the face o' the earth. Only yesterday did all the pieces begin to fall into place. They say the best place to hide somethin' is in plain sight and they must be right cause we knew all about you but figured it was as the Nashs said; you were the daughter of Robert Nash and for some reason he didn't want ya. I shoulda known from the start there was more to it than that. You were hiding real good until you made your first mistake. There ain't no girl in the world who knows those moves you tried on Cliff when you were tryin' to get away. Yeah I talked to Cliff, went to the jail the night he was arrested and talked to him through the window. He told me you reminded him o' our sister, that you knew some special techniques to try and get away from him that only a Luther could o' known and now I find he was right."

LooAnne could feel more tears gathering in the back of her eyes but she would not let herself cry in front of her brother; she could not be weak in his presence. Masking her emotions LooAnne's face hardened as she stared at her brother in anger and despair. Old feelings began to resurface and she realized that she had nothing to lose. She had to free Peter at all costs but that was something LooAnne Nash could never do, only Beth Luther could. LooAnne locked eyes with her brother, outwardly calm but inwardly praying frantically for deliverance.

"Alright so you figured out the secret," she confronted. "Did you also figure out how to bring back the clan from the dead where my uncle and I put them?"

Will's smirk faded into a jeering sneer as LooAnne

aroused his anger. "How dare you talk like that to me!" he yelled.

Hope filled LooAnne as she realized she had been in a very similar situation before. Only a few years' prior her cousin Carter had come to take her and her uncle as a peace offering to the rest of the Luther's who had disowned him. In the same stables, almost the same positions they had stood with Carter holding tightly to Ricky's young ward as hostage just as Will now held Peter. LooAnne had angered him to such an extent that he fired on her and alerted the guards to come to their aid. To LooAnne's great relief Amarie had diverted Carter's bullet, saving LooAnne's life. Now, however, Peter was in no position to save her, but LooAnne didn't need saving so long as Peter was spared. If she could anger her brother enough she was sure he would act on hatred and shoot her, bringing the guards and ranch hands to save Peter. She could only pray they would come in time before Will shot the deputy and made a run for it!

Armed with the acceptance of her own death and the knowledge of her brother's weaknesses LooAnne put her plan into action.

"I'll talk to you any way I want, Will Luther," she snapped. "You don't own me anymore, I'm not your toy to be played with."

Will was choking on fury upon hearing these words of defiance but LooAnne wasn't done yet.

"Every day of my childhood you tormented me! You and Cliff and all our cousins and aunts and uncles and even our father; every one of you mistreated Benjamin and I! You treated us like your own personal slaves and told us we weren't worth the dirt you made us crawl on. Well I'd like

170

you to take a look at your worthless little sister now. I'm
the niece and heiress of the Nash fortune, well respected in
society, well educated, and loved by many people."

"Rick Nash isn't many people!" Will yelled, "And as I
recall the first fella who came along dumped you for
another woman. Yeah we heard about that, it was all over
the papers! 'Kyle Denson leaves LooAnne Nash after
unruly bout with her uncle over inheritance'. So you see
you *are* worthless just like I said you were! No man will
ever love you!"

"That's a lie!" Peter's hoarse yet commanding voice broke
into Will's as he could no longer contain his rage. "You're
a liar, Will Luther. I love her!"

The stables were plunged into silence as LooAnne looked
up at Peter, her burdened heart suddenly lightening as
though it could take flight. He *loved* her? *How can he say
that?* She wondered. *How can he love me when I'm the
reason for all this?*

As if he could read her thoughts Peter continued,
"LooAnne, I don't care who you are or who you were. I
don't care how much money your uncle has or whether or
not you're ever gonna get it. I don't care if we never make
it a day past this one, and I don't care what I have to go
through to get you, I want you. I know I'm an idiot to say
this so soon after I first met you but..." Peter glanced at
Will, "...I might not get another chance."

LooAnne's eyes filled with tears as she listened to Peter's
words. Peter Andrews, a young deputy sheriff who had
come to her rescue and been swept up in her life with the
turn of every corner, who's quiet nature and deep thoughts
had been her own form of reassurance during their
imprisonment; a young man who had stolen her heart

when she vowed to never give it up again; he loved her despite it all and LooAnne felt her heart fill with joy...but only for a moment.

Will Luther snorted, "Well ain't that nice," he derided. "This worthless young lawman thinks he's in love with you! Too bad I gotta kill you, ain't it!" Will shoved Peter to the ground and raised his gun on LooAnne, ready to end her life!

LooAnne stood before him unwavering, praying that the guards would come for Peter, and a small part of her asking God to spare her own life as well.

"No, Luther, don't!" Peter cried desperately.

Will paused and looked down at the young deputy, "Why not? Do you know the trouble she caused when she ran away? The hours I was forced to search for her cause she could o' been squealin' our secrets to any lawmen in the county? Do you know the trouble I got into every night when I come back empty handed? No you don't! She never should o' been born to grow up and have all our family killed in the street! I only wish I had killed her sooner!" With that Will Luther pulled the trigger and nothing could be heard over the deafening sound of the gunshot!

FIFTEEN

Emotions Arise

The shot was loud, an ear-splitting bang that bounced off the walls and sounded through the pastures, drawing the attention of every occupant and staff member of the Nash Estate, though none of them knew what had just taken place.

Peter's heart sank as he watched Will Luther fire on LooAnne who stood helplessly before him! For a moment all he could do was watch from the floor as the pistol jumped back in Will's hand and LooAnne closed her eyes against an unavoidable death! Peter watched, waiting for the bullet to pierce LooAnne's chest and end her life in one horrific moment...

LooAnne stood, her eyes shut tightly, hands clenched at her side as she waited to feel the pain that was sure to come before she took her last breath. But it never did. As the sound of the gunshot slowly faded before them, LooAnne carefully opened her eyes, half expecting to see darkness, but was met with the confused face of her elder brother and the smoking barrel of his pistol. Carefully, almost hesitantly, LooAnne drew in a breath, filling her lungs with the stench of the stables and realizing that she was still alive!

The next moments flew buy in a blur of confusion and desperate prayers as Will turned to run! Peter stuck his foot under the fleeing murderer's legs, causing him to fall to the ground as the pistol flew from his hands! LooAnne, still a bit dazed and without the full knowledge of what she was doing, made a mad dash for the weapon, laying her foot on top of her brother's hand as he reached it! Will looked up at her, his eyes filled with fury and hatred, before he grabbed her ankle in his free hand and twisted it just enough that he was able to pull the gun from beneath her weight!

Will desperately trained his weapon on her once more, taking his final chance to be rid of his estranged sister once and for all, and a shot was fired but not by Will's gun! The enraged Luther let out a cry, his eyes widening as he stared up at LooAnne before falling limp at his sister's feet!

LooAnne clapped a hand over her mouth, stepping away from her brother's body as she looked up to see who had killed him. And there, standing in the stable door with a Winchester in his only good hand, was Stephen Parker! Letting the gun fall from his hold Stephen's eyes glazed over with sadness as he stared at LooAnne. "You lied to me," he whispered, his gaze boring into her soul. "You told me you would get us both out. You told me you would never leave me alone! You're a liar Elizabeth Luther!" LooAnne shook her head desperately as her eyes filled with tears, but Stephen turned and ran from the stables before she could plead with him.

"Stephen!" Peter called but it was of no use. LooAnne knew she had hurt her brother beyond forgiveness and this reality, mingling with the tensity of the moment and moments so recently passed, caused LooAnne's barrier to break.

Tears fell freely, escaping her eyes as though they were a dam waiting to break. LooAnne let out a cry and dropped to her knees by the body of her brother just as the stable doors were thrown open and anxious voices surrounded her. She heard the worried questions from the house staff and ranch hands mingled with their gasps and quiet murmuring, shouts for assistance and orders to call the sheriff and doctor, but her mind was so twisted and full of mixed sorrow and joy she tuned it all out. The thought of her twin brother hating her, the thought of Peter being hurt, the reality that she had been the cause of it all and more; it was all too much.

Only a few seconds later she felt a familiar pair of strong arms around her, lifting her up and carrying her away. At this point LooAnne could not have cared less where she was being taken for she trusted Peter who had apparently been loosed by one of the ranch hands. LooAnne buried her face in his chest, closing her eyes against the tears and sudden light that hit them as they exited the stables. Peter was dirty and his torn shirt wet with sweat but she didn't seem to notice as her mind began to wrap itself around the words that he was speaking.

"LooAnne, it's alright," his voice held a tremor she had never heard in it before, a small hint of the fear that he had felt upon nearly seeing her be killed. "It's all over now. Stephen's just upset, he'll come back."

LooAnne wanted to believe that, she wanted to believe that the only brother she had left in the world would come back without a hatred for her, but she could not, she knew it wasn't true.

LooAnne held onto Peter tightly as he carried her to the house, all the while hearing the distinct sound of her uncle's voice as he barked orders at his confused staff. She heard him tell Peter to take her into the study and she knew she had to get control of her crying, already feeling foolish for breaking down in front of Peter. *Peter,* she thought. He had professed his love for her and yet she doubted that he felt anything but pity. *How could he love me after all I've done?* she wondered silently.

By this time, they had reached the study and Peter sat LooAnne on the sofa before stepping back and allowing her uncle to kneel before her. Ricky laid a gentle hand on her shoulder as she tried to control her breathing.

"LooAnne, do you need a doctor?" he asked, his voice filled with concern.

His niece shook her head as she tried to breathe deeply, muffling a sob with the back of her hand.

"Are you sure?" Ricky asked.

LooAnne nodded, "I-I'm al-r-right, U-Uncle Ricky," she managed to say.

She could feel her heart, which was pounding vigorously against her chest, begin to slow and the tears lessen as she tried to wipe them away with her hand.

Ricky seemed to relax a bit as her hysterics came to a slow. He turned to one of the maids who had followed them down the hall and asked for a glass of water. Peter stood to the side, watching LooAnne intently yet quietly, his face etched with an expression LooAnne could not read as she caught his eyes for a moment before her uncle handed her the water. She drank it slowly, feeling the cooling liquid calm her a bit as it cleared the knot in her throat.

As her crying ceased she could see both her uncle and Peter sigh with relief before Ricky asked, "Are you sure you're alright? You're not hurt?"

LooAnne shook her head as her eyes met with Peter's, taking in the hidden look of pain and worry behind them. It was then that she realized the poor shape he was in; a result of the fight he had had with her brother. His face was marked with bruises and welts, streaked with dirt and sweat. His parched lips were cut, chipping with dried blood that had run down his chin and soaked his collar. His uniform was torn to nothing but filthy rags and LooAnne knew that Will had not given him any type of nourishment since they had been taken. She was amazed that he had been able to carry her all the way from the stables to the house without collapsing from exhaustion.

"Peter, you need a doctor," her voice was hoarse and dull from crying but carried just enough worry that her uncle turned his attention to the young deputy's endangered state.

Peter shook his head but Ricky spoke up before he could protest, "Yes you do, son," he agreed. "Why don't you take a seat and Chris will call the doctor?"

"I already did, sir," came Chris' voice, surprising LooAnne for she did not know he was in the room. "He and the sheriff should be here very shortly."

Ricky nodded, "Thank you, Chris. Why don't you take Deputy Andrews upstairs and see if you can get him comfortable until they arrive?"

"I don't want to cause no more trouble, sir," Peter objected.

"Nonsense," Ricky scolded. "You saved LooAnne's life on

more than on occasion, I owe you ten times more than I'll ever be able to pay."

Peter shook his head, "You don't owe me anything, Mr. Nash. It was a joy to do." Peter glanced at LooAnne and she thought she detected a small smile before he disappeared through the door with Chris Block.

Ricky immediately turned his full attention on his niece, taking her shoulder in his hands gently.

"LooAnne, don't lie to me, are you sure you're alright? I still think the doctor should look you over when he comes."

LooAnne only shook her head, no longer able to restrain herself from throwing her arms around her uncle as they both sank to the floor. She buried her face in his shoulder as he wrapped his arms around her, holding her close in an attempt to comfort her aching heart.

LooAnne could cry no more, her tears had run out and now all she could do was sit in her uncle's embrace, realizing how close she had come to never feeling it again. LooAnne closed her eyes and inhaled the calming sent of his cologne, allowing her tense muscles to relax. They sat in silence on the carpeted floor in front of the sofa for what seemed like a long while before LooAnne finally spoke quietly into her uncle's shoulder, "I don't know what to feel anymore," she admitted. "Will's dead, Cliff soon will be once he's convicted of Bill Morrison's murder, and Stephen hates me, not to mention the brother I lost last year. To think that if my parent's situation had been different I might have four loving brothers...I just can't imagine-"

"LooAnne," Ricky's kind voice kept his niece from going on, "Don't dwell on the past, my dear. It does no good to think back to things you wish had been when they're not. You don't know what kind of life you and your brothers would have lived had your parents not made the choices they did."

"I might not know exactly but I do know that it would have been much different. So many things would have been different even if I hadn't been stupid enough to leave so many years ago. Had I stayed with Ben like I promised none of this -"

"Now wait a minute," Ricky pulled away from his niece, holding her at arm's length as he looked into her reddened eyes. "Had you not left the Luther Estate when you were a little girl things would indeed be different, but not necessarily different in a good way. I know it's hard now, but do you not see how it was all worked together? Had you not been given the knowledge of the Luther's scheming minds and hateful hearts they might not be behind bars now. Had you not known how to defeat them last year they would not have been defeated. If it weren't for you there would be no Nash heir, no one to carry on our name, no one for me to love like my own child. Had you not left the Luther Estate I would be a very lonely man." Ricky looked down and LooAnne frowned, detecting a bit of something she did not understand in her uncle's expression, but before she could question him he went on. "LooAnne, there was a point in my life, many years before I met you, that left me a very stricken man. One day I'll tell you more of the matter but for right now I want you to know that had it not been for you coming into my very lonely life I would not have lasted much longer." LooAnne's frown deepened as she listened, but however curious she was, she did not want to upset her uncle by inquiring, she knew he would tell her in his own time. Ricky looked up at her and smiled wanly. "And if by some miracle I had survived to the more recent years I would still not be here today. As you well know, you were the one who pulled me from the estate years ago when it burned. You have done me so much good it's beyond anyone's understanding. What I owe Peter Andrews is not half of what I owe you. I know that I've little reason to convince you that you made the right decision in leaving but let me tell you this; you were a child when you decided to run from the people who were treating you wrongly. You left them, which took great courage, and somehow came across a sad, lonely man who just happened to be your uncle, only to later save his life and many others by being the key to jailing the Luther's. Now do you think that was all just coincidence? That it was all the result of a mistake?" Ricky shook his head, "Everything that happened was all part of a greater plan, LooAnne, every person's life is all part of a greater plan, a perfect plan. Our heavenly Father knows what He's doing and there is nothing we can do to stop the completion of His great arrangement. He foresaw it all and arranged it *exactly* how it should be."

As LooAnne's mind absorbed all that Ricky had said she was reminded of Peter's very similar words when they were held prisoner at the Luther Estate. *"Everything that's happened, whether it be over the last seven years or the last seven hours, is a part of His plan and the good thing about it is, His plan is perfect."*

And LooAnne knew for a fact that they were both very right. All that had happened over the course of her life had been a part of what the Almighty had intended for her since before she was even born; and now, with the death of her greatest adversary, all that was left to finally end the Luther war was to make amends with the only brother she had left. LooAnne only hoped that he would find it in his heart to forgive her.

"I have to talk to Stephen," she whispered, looking up at her uncle. "But he's probably long gone by now."

Ricky gave his niece a half smile, "We'll find him. If he's anything like his mother, he'll come around."

LooAnne returned her uncle's smile and nodded, "I've got to go find him."

LooAnne started to rise but her uncle took hold of her hand to stop her. "Let him be for a bit. He's got to get things right in his own mind."

"But I've got to apologize and explain why I left him," LooAnne protested.

"I know, but it's his decision whether or not he wants that explanation. Give him some time, I highly doubt he's still on the property anyways. If he wants your friendship, he'll have to come for it."

"How can he want my friendship after the way I've treated him? If I don't go after him and try to explain he'll hate me for the rest of our lives!"

"LooAnne, you must remember he's a Luther. He might be your brother but you don't know him as well as you once did. If he never comes back, then maybe that's just as well."

"How can you say that?" LooAnne exclaimed, "He's the only immediate family I have left."

A grin suddenly broke on Ricky's face, confusing LooAnne until he spoke, "So you do want your brother back after all?"

LooAnne could not help but mirror her uncle's expression. "Yes," she was finally able to admit, "I do want him back. After Mama died he was the only thing I had left at that place."

It was this thought that caused LooAnne to frown, "And I was the only one he had and I abandoned him."

Ricky shook his head, "You were a child, LooAnne, you did what you could at the time. You said he was weak, he might not have been able to travel all that way, he might have gotten you both caught and you know what would have happened in that case?"

LooAnne nodded, "I might have never gotten the chance to escape again."

"And neither of you would be here now."

"But he might have been able to make it," LooAnne mused. "I just never gave him the chance."

"What's done is done, LooAnne. You don't know what would have happened if you tried to take him with you but it doesn't matter. Both you and your brother are now safe from the Luther's, all you have to do is make amends with each other if he's willing. And until he comes back, we'll just have to wait."

"What if he doesn't come back, Uncle Ricky?" LooAnne asked sorrowfully. "What if I never see him again?"

Ricky nodded sadly, "That is an unfortunate possibility, one we must accept. All we can do is pray that he sees the need to make things right."

Though it hurt LooAnne to hear she saw the wisdom in her uncle's words and agreed with a nod, praying that Stephen would return soon.

It was not long after that Sheriff Murphy and Dr. Abrams arrived. The doctor took a quick look at LooAnne per her uncle's insistence and assured them both that she was fine, only suffering from minor shock. He was then taken upstairs to examine Peter who was not given such a good report. Dr. Abrams was forced to stitch many of the young deputy's wounds and said that he had suffered from malnutrition and dehydration but nothing too severe that a few days' rest and good food would not heal.

Ricky insisted upon the young man staying at the estate as long as he wanted and had Chris call the Andrews' to tell them their son had been recovered and was, for the most part, alright.

After her examination Sheriff Murphy asked LooAnne to give him a detailed report of the incident that had taken place that afternoon. She told him about going out to the stables and finding Will Luther there with Peter Andrews under the threat of his pistol. She told him how Will had grown angry at her protests without letting on exactly what she had said to him.

"He fired a shot right at me," LooAnne related, staring down into the dark fireplace as she recalled the moment of terror and confusion. "I closed my eyes and thought for sure I would be dead the next second, but I felt nothing and when I opened them again we were just staring at each other. I don't know what happened, he couldn't have missed at point-blank range."

Sheriff Murphy scratched his chin, perplexed. "We'll examine the gun he used, it might have misfired. What happened after that?"

"He turned to run and Peter tripped him. I was so disoriented I didn't really know what I was doing. Will fell and I saw the gun fly from his hand and knew I had to get it before he did. We reached it simultaneously and I ended up with my foot on top of his hand. He grabbed my ankle and yanked the gun out from under me, he was about to shoot when Stephen killed him from the doorway."

Sheriff Murphy nodded as he jotted down LooAnne's words on his note pad. "And where is Mr. Parker at the moment?"

LooAnne glanced at her uncle who was standing to the side listening intently before saying, "Um, I believe he was a little shaken by the experience and ran off. I'm not sure where he is."

Sheriff Murphy nodded, "Well your story and Andrews' were in perfect cynic so I see no reason to bother Mr. Parker." the sheriff stood and shook LooAnne's hand. "We'll get Luther's body off your property and file our report. You'll have to come testify against Ray but other than that the case is closed."

LooAnne smiled gratefully at Matt Murphy. "I really do appreciate it, Sheriff."

"And so do I," Ricky added.

"I'm just glad we finally have more o' them Luther's behind bars. I know it must be hard on you, Mr. Nash considering they're kin and all but-"

Ricky shook his head, "It is what it is, Matt. I assure you I'm just as relieved as you are."

Ricky and LooAnne walked with Sheriff Murphy to the entry hall expressing again their thanks for all he had done. He was just about to leave when one of the police officers came running from the stables to the house, "Take a look at this, Sheriff!" he said, handing Matt Murphy Will's gun. "It looks like it's jammed."

Sheriff Murphy examined the gun and nodded, "It certainly does. This must be the reason you weren't killed,

Miss Nash," he said, turning to LooAnne. "This is one o' them Colt 380 hammerless guns, the bullets come outta the clip and can get jammed every now and then. It saved your life."

LooAnne looked first at the gun and then at her uncle before turning her attention back to Matt Murphy, "So what you're saying is if this gun hadn't jammed just when it did I'd be dead?"

The sheriff nodded, "No doubt o' that, ma-am. Possibly Peter Andrews as well, not to mention Will Luther would o' gotten away."

Ricky and LooAnne looked at each other, both of them thinking the same thing.

"I recon I'll see you both later," the sheriff said as he shook Ricky's hand and left.

Her uncle looked down at LooAnne and shook his head in amazement. "I have the slightest feeling the Almighty isn't done with you, my dear."

LooAnne nodded, her eyes still planted on where the gun had lain in the sheriff's hand, realizing how close she had come to dying and the miracle that had occurred to save her life!

Ricky too, realized how close he had come to losing his niece, in both the stable incident and to the Luther's evil scheme to get revenge on him for being a significant part in the death and imprisonment of many of their family members. He could not imagine the horrifying situation they would now be in had it not been for Peter Andrews. He wanted, somehow, to repay the young deputy for all he had done but knew that there was no amount of money or property that could express his gratefulness.

After contacting Mr. and Mrs. Andrews, Chris conveyed to

his employer their joy upon learning that their son had been found. The steward said he expected the couple to arrive at the estate sometime after dinner, saying that they were both most anxious to see Peter. Ricky had rooms prepared for them to stay the night and any following days that they wished.

Immediately after the sheriff left, LooAnne, feeling fatigued and in need of solitude, told her uncle that she was going to get freshened up and hastened to her room. The events of the afternoon overwhelmed her and she could not take her mind from Peter's heartfelt speech in the stable barn. She wondered if he had only said those things because he thought death was inevitable and felt sorry for her having to stand there and listen to her brother's hateful words. She could not help but think that his feelings had, or soon would, change. These thoughts, mixed with worry and fear over Stephen, caused LooAnne to feel extremely disheartened. Though Will was dead, and Cliff and Ray behind bars, she could not help but feel that this was far from over...

SIXTEEN

Love and Lies

In the following hours LooAnne tried her best to sleep but found her mind, and indeed her heart, too occupied for rest. She could not forget the words Peter had spoken moments before their averted death. He had looked and sounded so sincere that a part of her could not help but cry out to believe him. But neither could she forget what Kyle had done, the way he had left her for Amarie Hearten after three years of faithful waiting. LooAnne could not forget how he used Ricky's young, naive ward to marry and get her money when he had already pledged his fidelity to LooAnne herself. Now she could not help but fear that Peter would lie to her as well, and want her not for love but for what Kyle had wanted, money.

Her emotions ached for an answer not only in the matters of her heart, but in the matter of her brother. LooAnne knew very well that the chances of having him back were few and far between but she could not help but want, if not his love, then his good favor. Once Cliff faced execution for Bill's murder, Stephen would be the only brother she had left, the only brother that had ever been worth having.

Why did I leave him alone? She asked herself as she lay on her bed staring at the brown ceiling above her. *Why should I have thought that he would grow up to be like them when he never was?* LooAnne's mind and conscience would not let her forget what she supposed to be the worst mistake of her life. She wished beyond even her own understanding that she could go back and change it all; that she could have gotten her brother out and taken him with her instead of breaking her promise and leaving him alone to face the cruelty of their family. But now it was too late. LooAnne feared that she would never see Stephen again and that he would run into a world he thought he had to face with the same cruelty and vengeance he was shown as a child. LooAnne shivered at this thought of her brother turning into a criminal because of what she had done. Though it might not have been her fault that Will and Cliff came back for revenge, there was no way to avoid blame for Stephen's corrupted childhood, and perhaps his corrupted adulthood as well!

LooAnne's troubling thoughts were interrupted by the sound of voices in the study directly below her. LooAnne stood from the bed and crossed the room to a small vent in the floor installed to allow heat from the fireplace bellow to warm her bedroom. From there she could hear all that went on in the first floor room, but, not wanting to eavesdrop, she decided to see who it was and listen no more. LooAnne stood directly above the vent and peered down through its metal bars at a small portion of her uncle's desk. She heard his familiar voice and that of a woman whom she recognized instantly as Mrs. Andrews!

"I don't know how to thank you, Mr. Nash," the lady's kindly voice spoke, filled with gratefulness. "We've been scared half out of our minds!"

"I don't blame you in the slightest, Mrs. Andrews," Ricky said. "Mr. Block will take you all upstairs to see Peter. The doctor said he would recover quickly and fully but needs his rest for the next few days. He said he would be by in a couple of days to check the stitches and tend to any bandages that might need changing."

"Thank you, sir. We're mighty beholdin' to you," came Mr. Andrews' deep baritone.

"Oh no, it's my pleasure. Were it not for your son my niece wouldn't be here, this is the least I can do."

LooAnne decided to listen to no more of their conversation and walked away from the vent to the door, knowing they would come upstairs at any moment. She stood just inside it, waiting to hear their steps on the stairs as they ascended. Soon she heard the many footsteps as the guests climbed the stairs and to her surprise LooAnne could also make out the very distinct voice of Clara Andrews. She had supposed that they left her at home to tend to the house but now that she was here a sudden thought struck LooAnne; what should happen if Stephen returned while Clara was there? LooAnne was at a loss to know what kind of situation they would find themselves in should a meeting such as that take place. She didn't want Clara to be hurt and yet, if her brother was the upright man she hoped him to be, LooAnne wondered if the young maid might forgive him for his secrecy and be reunited with the man she loved? And if she could somehow find Stephen, LooAnne wondered if it might be a means to get him to come back to the estate long enough for her to ask him for forgiveness!

But her hopes of finding Stephen were all but gone the

moment he had left. LooAnne knew that he could be anywhere in the state, putting miles between them as the minutes passed. *There's no way I could ever find him,* she realized. Now her only hope was that Stephen would see fit to come back and make amends...or maybe he would come back for Clara!

LooAnne listened as Mr. Block showed the Andrews family into Peter's room not far down the hall. She could not help but smile at the cry of joy from Mrs. Andrews when she saw her son alive. She was sure they were all equally glad to be reunited, and she could not help but wish that she, herself, could be reunited with her brother. Now all she could do was pray that the Lord protected him and lead him down the path to his own life, whether it be back to the Nash Estate or further away.

Time passed quickly and soon dinner was ready. LooAnne freshened up before joining her uncle in the dining room where she also found Mr. and Mrs. Andrews and their daughter; all of whom expressed their kind thankfulness at her safe return. LooAnne thanked them for their words and then the meal commenced. Ricky spoke endlessly with Mr. Andrews on many a business matter and situations at Belle Hall. Clara and LooAnne found themselves in deep conversation as well, mainly relating to her kidnapping though LooAnne did not mention to the young maid of Stephen's involvement in the plot for revenge.

After the meal was finished LooAnne finally felt the lack of sleep from the previous night and the emotional and physical struggles of that day begin to wear on her. Mrs. Andrews and her daughter had gone upstairs to check on Peter, and Ricky and Mr. Andrews were still in the midst of their conversation.

LooAnne laid her napkin on the table and excused herself, saying she was going to bed early. After saying goodnight to her uncle and Mr. Andrews, LooAnne climbed the stairs to her bedroom where the soft bed immediately called to her as if asking her to crawl between it's comforting sheets. LooAnne changed into her night clothes, turned off the lamp and shut the curtains, not allowing the bit of light from the setting sun to disturb her sleep. She then climbed beneath the embroidered comforter and lacy sheets, feeling all the tensity of the past twenty-four hours momentarily drain away as her head hit the pillow and she fell off into a deep sleep...

...All was dark, LooAnne could hear nothing but the faded hum of angry voices but seemed unable to find their source. Suddenly she was back in the stables, face to face with her brother as he pointed his gun at her! Confused, LooAnne wanted to run but was frozen as her mind whirled with fear!
Will Luther snorted, "Well ain't that nice," he derided, his voice seeming far away though he stood only a few feet from her. "This worthless young lawman thinks he's in love with you!"
LooAnne instantly realized that Peter was also there, beaten and bruised on the floor, helpless against her brother!
"Too bad I gotta kill you, ain't it!" Will raised his gun on LooAnne, ready to end her life!
"No, Luther, don't!" Peter cried desperately.
Will paused and looked down at the young deputy, "Why not?" he sneered. "She never should o' been born to grow up and have all our family killed in the street! I only wish I

had killed her sooner!" With that Will pulled the trigger and nothing could be heard over the deafening sound of the gunshot!

In an instant LooAnne was awake! She shot up in bed, gasping for air as though she were about to take her last breath! She sat frozen for a moment, staring blankly at the dark room in front of her; trying to resolve what had happened.

"It was just a dream," she whispered to herself, letting out a sigh of relief. LooAnne felt a trickle of sweat roll down the back of her neck. She looked to her side and squinted at the clock, seeing that it was almost two in the morning. LooAnne let out a breath and laid back down, feeling the sweat on her neck soak into her feather pillow. She knew that the chances of getting back to sleep were nearly nonexistent. Every time she closed her eyes vivid memories of her dream passed through her mind and she was forced to throw them open again to rid herself of the horrifying moment. LooAnne sighed as she stared at the ceiling, trying to occupy her mind with any other thought she could imagine.

She was in the midst of the pleasant recollection of Peter's confessed love when her mind was otherwise distracted by a sudden clanging noise from the vent across the room! As soon as it started it had stopped and all was plunged into silence once more though now it was an eerie silence as if something in the house were amiss! LooAnne slowly sat up, listening for any following noises to assure her that it was only her uncle getting up to fetch something, but all remained quiet which compelled LooAnne to rise from the bed and cross the room, intrigued as to what had caused the clatter...or who!

Walking silently across the floor, LooAnne approached the vent and knelt next to it quietly, peering through the thin metal bars into the study just as she had done earlier.

She saw that the lamp on top of the desk was on, lighting the small corner of the room which was all that could be seen. LooAnne did, however, catch the shadow of a man as he moved about in the study!

LooAnne frowned deeply as she tried to look closer, wondering what her uncle would be doing up at this time of night?

I hope he's not sick, LooAnne mused. She decided to go downstairs and make certain that her uncle was not unwell, knowing it was very unusual for him to be up at such an hour.

LooAnne donned her robe, stuffing her arms into it as she opened her bedroom door and walked out into the upper hall. She approached the stairs and could see the dim light casting a small bit of shadow on the hallway at the foot of the stairs. LooAnne descended slowly, not wanting to wake anyone with the creaking of the steps. When she reached the bottom she could hear her uncle shuffling through what sounded like papers in his desk drawer. The study door was open but not enough for her to discern what her uncle was doing.

Unaware of what she was about to be faced with, LooAnne pushed open the study door, "Uncle Ricky, is something wrong?"

The room was dark, all except the corner where the lamp stood. Papers, documents, and folders of all kinds lay strewn on her uncle's desk.

The figure who was bent over the desk shuffling anxiously

through its contents, turned to face her, and to LooAnne's dismay it was not her uncle!

He was much thinner and very broad; his face hidden in the shadow of the room where LooAnne could see only its outline; all she needed to see to know instantly who it was! LooAnne let a gasp escape her as she took a step back, her heart immediately beginning to race!

"*Stephen*!" she exclaimed in a whisper, unable to speak any higher for the shock that pulsed through her!

For a moment they stood frozen, both of them staring at the other in paralyzed unease. It was, indeed, the young Luther; still wearing the clothes Chris had lent him, his arm still wrapped in a sling. LooAnne could not believe that he was standing before her and in the act of robbing her uncle!

Stephen was the first of the two to make a move; to LooAnne's alarm and dismay he pulled a pistol from his belt and pointed it directly at his sister!

"Don't get in my way, Miss Nash," he hissed in a cold, warning voice. "You caused me enough pain and heartache to last a lifetime, now I suggest you get right back up them stairs and forget I'm here!"

Out of shock LooAnne took a step back, her eyes widening as she looked at the gun her brother now held on her!

"St-Stephen, you can't mean this!" she whispered, though there was no denying that her brother was capable of killing her should he wish to.

The young Luther nodded, "Yes I can!" he stated firmly. "I'm a Luther and there ain't nothin' I can do about it. This is who I am; this is the way it's gotta be!"

"No!" LooAnne shook her head pleadingly, "It's doesn't

have to be this way! You're not like them!"

"How would you know? You left me for dead, what makes you think you know anything about who I really am?" Venom dripped mercilessly from Stephen's voice as he spoke; his words shooting daggers at LooAnne's heart. She felt a knot beginning to grow in her throat as she said a silent prayer.

"Stephen, please," LooAnne whispered, the light from the desk causing the tears in her eyes to glisten, "I made a mistake; a terrible one, but that is no reason for you to ruin your life!"

"My life is already ruined because of your mistake!" her brother snapped angrily. "My whole life has been a lost cause; you were the last chance I had. I realize now that my fate was sealed the minute you up and left me to die with the Luther's!"

"You're wrong, Stephen," LooAnne defended, "I might have made a mistake but there comes a time when every man must take responsibility for his own actions. No matter what any of your family has done, *you* are the one to make your own choices from now on and you will be held accountable for them whether you blame me or not. I know I left you, and I cannot tell you the regret I've felt for doing so, but I'm not the one who broke in here, I'm not the one trying to rob my uncle. That is a choice that you made and unless you stop it this instant you *will* pay for it!"

Stephen snorted as if amused, "I ain't gonna pay for nothin' I don't get caught doin', and you're not gonna tell nobody it was me!"

LooAnne swallowed the knot in her throat, knowing she had to stand up to her brother. "Benjamin Luther, unless you kill me I *will* tell. As much as I love you I can't let you get away with-."

"Love me?" Stephen's interruption was so loud that LooAnne was sure it had awakened many of the house occupants! Nevertheless, her brother continued, unable to control his anger any longer, "You never loved me! You left me all alone with people you knew would hurt me and never gave it a second thought! It's all your fault I never had the chance to get away!"

Before LooAnne could respond, the door to her uncle's bedroom, which was directly across the hall t the bottom of the stairs, opened, revealing a tired looking Ricky who was just pulling on his robe. The moment his eyes took in the scene before him they widened in both fear and shock. LooAnne had her doubts that Stephen would hurt her; she was, after all, his sister, and she could not forget the loving brother she had once known him to be. But she knew of his dislike for Ricky, a hatred drilled into him from childhood by the warped minds of the Luthers, and now she feared for her uncle's safety.

Ricky looked from his niece to Stephen and narrowed his eyes, "What's going on? Who are you?"

"Uncle Ricky, just please stay out of it," LooAnne begged, not looking back at her uncle for fear of taking her eyes off her brother.

"Why not tell him, Miss Nash?" Stephen derided. "I'm sure he knows about the worthless twin that you left behind to die!"

With this statement Ricky's eyes grew wider and he took a careful step towards his niece. "Ben Luther," he clarified aloud.

Stephen nodded, "The one and only. Now if you Nash's

196

would be so kind, I got things that need doin', so get outta my way!"

However afraid she was, LooAnne stood her ground, determined that her brother would not escape this time. She shook her head boldly, "I'll not let you leave, Stephen."

The young Luther raised his gun to LooAnne's forehead, "Then I'll have to get you outta my way!"

"You won't kill me," LooAnne spoke with great confidence, while every ounce of common sense within her protested.

Only a moment later the gun went off; the walls of the house compacting the ear-splitting sound! And for a second time that day LooAnne expected to feel the bullet pierce her as her hopes were momentarily dashed, but instead she felt it whiz past her head, lodging in the wall behind her!

"Next time I won't miss! Now move!" Stephen's voice was accompanied by the banging of doors throughout the house and LooAnne heard many footsteps running down the stairs behind her! Then a stunned voice cried out, "Stephen!"

LooAnne saw her brother's head instantly turn towards the stairs, his eyes thrown open in shock upon hearing the familiar exclamation.

"C-Clara," he whispered, his entire demeanor withering to shame.

"Stephen, what are you doing?" Clara cried.

LooAnne saw a look of sadness and hurt cross her brother's face as he stared at his supposed fiancé, and she knew that this might be the chance she had been looking for.

"Stephen," she whispered, drawing the wavering attention of her brother, "is this really what you want? If you do this, you'll be running for the rest of your life! You'll never be able to start over, you'll never be able to get a respectable job, or a good home, or...raise a family." Stephen glanced over at Clara who stood on the stairs behind her father, looking at him with sorrow in her eyes. "I know this isn't you," LooAnne continued, "this isn't who you really are. I might not have been there for seven years of your life but for the last two days I have. I've seen who you want to be versus who your brothers forced you to be and like I said before, the things your family – *our* family – did in the past do not have to dictate who we are in the future."

"You're wrong!" Stephen barked, looking LooAnne in the eye angrily, "You might have been able to escape it but I can't! I don't know anything else! I've been raised a killer and thief and now you expect me to turn around and forget it all! Forget everything they did to me, everything they taught me! Forget what you did to me when I trusted you with my life! How can I trust anyone anymore after the only person I had to rely on left me after she promised she never would?"

By this time LooAnne's tears were threatening to spill and she could detect a crack in Stephen's voice as he spoke in anguish. She knew that there was nothing she could do to make right what she had wronged, but she had to tell her brother what was in her heart before it was too late.

"Stephen, I don't expect you to forget any of those things. Up to this day I still can't. But I have no excuse as to why I left you other than to say that I was afraid. I was afraid I would take you with me and you wouldn't be able to make it; I was afraid I wouldn't be able to feed you or give you shelter; I was afraid we would get caught and you would be punished for my decision; and yes, I was afraid that you would grow up to be like our family."

By this time Chris, three of the four estate guards, and many members of the house staff had come running, drawn by Stephen's warning gunshot. LooAnne knew that she had an audience but no matter what knowledge they learned that night, she could not let her brother escape without knowing that she still loved him.

Stephen stood silently, staring at LooAnne with mixed emotions twisting his expression. The all too familiar eyes of her brother caused LooAnne to look down as she continued, feeling his intent stare upon her as she spoke. "At the time I was so young and afraid, I hardly knew what I was doing," she admitted, "I just wanted to get away. Already they hated me, they treated us both so badly I couldn't take it anymore and then I remembered what my father had told me the night he died, he told me I had to get out. The last words Papa said to me were commands to get away from the very family he had forced us all to endure since we were born. That was what made up my mind, that was when I knew I had to escape. I wanted to take you, I swear I did, but when that night came and I watched you laying there sleeping I couldn't bring myself to wake you and drag you into a life in which I didn't know if I could keep you alive." LooAnne finally looked up at her brother, tears coating her dark brown eyes. "But I promise you it was the hardest thing I've ever done in my life. To leave you there alone, knowing that I would most likely never see you again..."

"But you didn't love me enough to stay," Stephen

whispered, no longer angry but stricken with sorrow, "The one person I thought loved me didn't even care enough not to leave."

LooAnne felt a tear leak from her eye and roll slowly down her cheek. "No," she shook her head, locking eyes with her brother, "I didn't leave you because I didn't love you, I left you because I *did*; because in leaving I was risking my life and I had no right to risk yours as well. But you had every right to make that decision for yourself and I didn't give you that chance; for that I am sorrier than I can say. But I promise you, Benjamin Luther, I did *not* leave because I didn't love you, I never stopped loving you. As a child you were the only thing worth loving in my entire world and no matter what, I can never forget that."

Stephen looked at LooAnne, his eyes filled with tears which he refused to let fall. Could he really believe all she had said? Had she actually wanted him back this entire time? He then looked beyond her at her uncle – *their* uncle. Was he really the man his niece had claimed him to be? Would he really try his best to help his estranged nephew after all Stephen had done? The young Luther could not help but doubt. His eyes wandered from Ricky to Mr. Andrews and Clara. Stephen knew he had put them all through a terrible experience; one that nearly got their son and brother killed. He had lied to Clara and hid their relationship from her father, the very person who deserved to know. Now, looking at the faces of the people he had hurt, Stephen could not believe that any of them could find it in their hearts to forgive him. Despite what his sister said, it was already too late.

Stephen could look at Clara's tearful eyes no longer and

turned back to LooAnne. His pistol still aimed at his sister's head as though he intended to kill her. He sighed and shook his head sorrowfully, "Beth, it's too late," he whispered, his voice trembling. "After all I've done, there ain't no chance for me. I could never get a good job or raise a family. All I got is what the Luther's gave me, a thief's know-how, and that ain't enough to live the life you want me to live."

To Stephen's surprise his sister nodded, "You're right," she stated, "you don't have what it takes to live a good life, but neither do I; neither do any of these people in this room. Stephen, we can't do anything if the Heavenly Father doesn't help us. But I promise you He will; He'll help you live a good and wonderful life if that's what you want, but if it's not then that's your decision. I've done what I wanted to do, I told you how I feel; I love you like the brother you are and I want you to get to live this new life. I was a Luther too, I know how you feel and I know it's hard, but with God *nothing* will be impossible."

Stephen stared at LooAnne, his mind numb from the pain and anger he had lived all his life, but his heart full with his sister's words. He looked down at the pistol in his hand, a tool he had used to threaten his sister, and now he decided that henceforth he would use it to protect her as she had protected him.

His eyes softened as he lowered it, half expecting the guards to tackle him, but everyone stood frozen in place except LooAnne, who jumped into her brother's arms, holding him tightly for the first time in almost seven years. "I'm so sorry I left you," she whispered through her tears. "Please forgive me?"

Stephen shook his head, burying it in his sister's shoulder,

"I'll forgive you if you can forgive me?"

LooAnne nodded, "You're my brother, Ben Luther, I forgave you a long time ago!"

SEVENTEEN

Making Amends

With her brother's arms wrapped around her LooAnne closed her eyes, taking in the moment of contentment. Finally, after so many years of fearing the worst and knowing she was to blame, she was finally able to embrace her brother again and the feeling gratified her. Like LooAnne, Stephen too was making the most of their tearful reunion. Holding his sister close; allowing the reality to hit him. All this time his lost sister had been right under his nose. The niece and heiress of Rick Nash; the alleged daughter of his younger brother, was Beth Luther. She had been hiding her true identity for years and it surprised Stephen that they had done it without the knowledge of the Luthers. But now, he realized, as he opened his eyes and was met with the shocked stares of his uncle, the Andrews' and the house staff, his sister's secret could not be kept for much longer!

LooAnne, too, had realized this disturbing fact. Slowly she pulled away from Stephen and turned to face the gathered audience. Mr. Andrews and his daughter were standing on the bottom few stairs with Mrs. Andrews and Peter at the top as though she had prevented him from joining the fight due to his fragile condition. Almost the entire house staff was present, looking on in shock. LooAnne cast her uncle a pleading look to end the moment of awkward silence and send his workers away.

Ricky, having already thought of such a speech, turned to his employees and addressed them with firmness, though they knew inwardly he implored, "After what you all have seen I feel it necessary to confirm your suspicions. It is true that LooAnne is not Robert's daughter; she is the daughter of my sister Amanda and her husband, Jason Luther, but nevertheless she is my niece and I love her very much. This secret, should it be known to the wrong people, could prove very dangerous. Not all the Luthers are dead or imprisoned and I have many an enemy who would love the get their hands on such a story. I would like to ask that you say nothing to anyone about what's happened. I can't stop any of you from telling but I ask that you do this not only for LooAnne, but for me as well. If you want to leave my employ then by all means do so, but please respect my wishes even beyond my home. As you have figured out, this is a tedious business and I don't want anyone else getting hurt. I do thank you for your evident concern and for responding so quickly. I couldn't ask for a finer bunch of workers than you all have proven yourselves to be. Now if you would please excuse us, my niece, nephew and I have quite a bit to discuss."

Without another word the on looking maids, guards, footman, butler, and valet turned and moved slowly back to their designated quarters, leaving Chris and the Andrews' standing in the hall with Ricky, LooAnne, and Stephen.

Ricky wasted no time in taking the situation in hand. Turning to Stephen he said, "Young man, I've no doubt that we all have much to discuss but before we proceed any further I would like to make one thing very clear; I highly dislike people who break into my home and threaten my niece, brother or no brother. I am willing to give you every chance to make a better impression of yourself but until then I suggest you tread lightly."

LooAnne wanted to protest her uncle's scolding but knew he was right. Stephen had not only broken into the estate but he had fired his gun at her! She did not, nor did she think she should, take such a matter lightly.

Stephen nodded rather nervously as he faced his uncle. "I understand, sir. I know what I did was wrong and I'll do my best to make it right."

Ricky nodded stiffly, "First thing I want to know is how you got in here past the guards."

Without hesitation Stephen reached into his trouser pocket and produced a very familiar bit of gold which he held in his palm for all to see. LooAnne gasped when she laid eyes on her small ring; the ring which granted its wearer access to the Nash Estate without question of the guards! Instantly she looked down at her finger and realized for the first time since they were kidnapped that it was gone! "You took that from me when I was unconscious!" she accused, indignant at the thought of her brother robbing her while she was helpless.

"I didn't, I swear I didn't," Stephen defended himself. "When Will saw it and realized what it was he took it. I knew it could mean trouble if he ever had the chance to use it so while he was sleepin' I got it outta his pocket."

LooAnne's face softened as Stephen placed the small ring in her hand. She was about to apologize when her expression suddenly frowned, "But then you used it for yourself," she pointed out.

Stephen looked down shamefully and nodded, "I'm awful sorry, I just needed some money to get out of the state."

"So instead of asking for it you decided to come in uninvited and steal it?" Ricky countered.

Stephen nodded hesitantly. "Yes, sir. I just figured you wouldn't want anything to do with me so it was the only way."

"Young man, you're my sister's son" Ricky stated, "if you need help I'll help you but stealing is stealing whether you need the money or not. Now if you're certain I can trust you I'll give you a job here at the estate until you get back on your feet and then if you wish to continue you may and if not that's fine too."

Stephen's face immediately lightened at his uncle's words, but Ricky was not yet finished. "However, if you give me any reason at all I *will* fire you, is that understood?"

Stephen's face sobered and he nodded vigorously, "I understand, sir. I promise I won't give you no reason to fire me! I'll be the best worker you ever had, Mr. Nash, I swear I will!"

Ricky nodded as though he believed his nephew would do just that, "Then you can go to work with the ranch hands as soon as your arm allows. We'll talk further on it in the morning."

Stephen nodded and shook his uncles hand gratefully, "I can't tell ya how much I appreciate this, sir. After what I did tonight I don't deserve a second chance."

"Everyone deserves a second chance, Stephen," Ricky assured, accepting his nephew's hand, "and you've got one so I suggest you use it wisely."

"I will, sir. I really am sorry for all the trouble I caused."

Ricky nodded, "And you've been forgiven. Chris will show you to the bunkhouse and Sam can find you a place to sleep for the night if you like?"

Stephen stole a quick glance at Clara before nodding, "That'd be right nice of you, sir."

Ricky nodded to Chris who started out the back door. Stephen expressed his apologies once more before bidding the group goodnight and following the steward out of the house. The moment they were out of sight Ricky sighed and turned to the Andrews', "I'm very sorry for all this. I know that my nephews, all of them, have caused you all a lot of trouble, and I can't begin to apologize for it."

"You don't need to apologize, sir," Mr. Andrews assured his employer. "We're just glad that it's all over and no one was seriously hurt." Peter's father then cast a glance at LooAnne before continuing, "And you can be sure your secret is safe with us. Miss Nash is a very fine young lady, Luther or not."

LooAnne smiled thankfully at Matt Andrews, "Thank you, Mr. Andrews. I thank you beyond words for saying so; and thank you for taking all this so well, I really do appreciate it."

"It's our pleasure, ma-am. Now if y'all would excuse us, we're gonna get back to bed."

Mr. Andrews headed upstairs, where his wife and son stood, the three of them disappearing into Peter's bedroom. Clara, however, her face creased with many emotions, turned to LooAnne and asked, "Forgive me, Miss Nash, but could I speak with you privately before you go to bed?"

LooAnne knew instantly that Clara was in want of an in-depth explanation as to how LooAnne was Stephen's sister when she had appeared not to know him when they met so briefly that night.

"Of course, Clara. We can talk in the study if it's alright with Uncle Ricky?"

Her uncle nodded, "Of course you may, my dear. I'm going back to bed, if you need anything come wake me."

LooAnne nodded as she pecked her uncle's cheek, "I will. Goodnight, Uncle Ricky."

"Goodnight, LooAnne; Clara."

Ricky then turned and disappeared through his bedroom door, leaving LooAnne and the young maid alone.

LooAnne showed Clara into the study and closed the door, asking her to have a seat. After the two were both seated LooAnne spoke first, "I know you must be very confused, Clara, but I promise you I had no idea at the time who Stephen really was."

Clara looked at the floor and shook her head, as if trying to get all the facts straight in her mind. "I-I just don't know what to think, Miss Nash. I thought something had happened to Stephen or that he had deserted me for a better life, and now to find out he's your brother and he was involved in *kidnapping* you! It's all so confusing and disturbing at the same time."

LooAnne nodded, "I know, it is for me too. You see I ran away from my family when I was very little and haven't seen my brothers at all since then. When I saw Benji – or Stephen I should say – that night you all met at Belle Hall I had no idea who he was. I recognized him only as someone I thought I had seen before but didn't know him as my brother partly because he had changed a lot but mostly because I had tried so hard to forget him. I had no idea I would ever see him again and at the time I had to protect myself somehow from the hurt of being separated from him. I really didn't know that your beau, Stephen was my brother, Ben. He's done a lot of things that he regrets, but I promise, you weren't one of them."

At mention of herself Clara looked up at LooAnne doubtfully.

"I'm telling you the truth," LooAnne assured her. "My brother loves you, he always has. After he was forced to take Peter and I, he thought he had lost you forever, and it crushed him. He was ready to give up, but the idea of having another chance with you kept him going. I can't make this decision for you, but if you still think that Stephen is the one God has for you, then I think you should give him another chance."

Clara looked at LooAnne as though she longed to believe her but there was something holding her back. "I really do want to, Miss Nash, but he's not the person he said he was, he's a – a..."

"A Luther," LooAnne finished.

Clara sighed and nodded, "I don't mean to offend -"

"You've not offended me, Clara, I completely understand," LooAnne assured. "And it's good to be cautious, especially about matters such as these. I just wanted you to know that Stephen loves you. All he did, meeting you in secret, not letting you tell anyone about him, and even kidnapping me and Peter, was all to protect you from his brothers."

Clara frowned, "It was?"

"It was," LooAnne nodded, "They threatened to hurt you if he didn't do everything they said. He was ready to give his own life to protect you from his brothers."

"Really, Miss Nash?" Clara's eyes were no longer dulled by stress and uncertainty but alive with hope.

LooAnne smiled, "Really."

"I – I don't know what to think," she admitted.

LooAnne leaned forward in her seat, looking the young maid in the eye, "Pray about it, Clara. God brought you and Stephen together for a reason and He'll show you what that reason is. As I said before, if you're meant for each other then he's worth waiting for."

After a moment of contemplation Clara's face was lit with a smile, "I'll talk to him in the morning! Oh thank you for everything, Miss Nash.

LooAnne returned Clara's smile, "You're very welcome, Clara. Thank you for not being angry with me after all that my family has done."

Clara shook her head, "No one should blame you for what your family has done, Miss Nash. You aren't them."

LooAnne stood and embraced the young maid gratefully. "Thank you, Clara. Even if I don't one day call you my sister I will never forget your kindness."

"And I won't ever forget yours, Miss Nash." Clara pulled away and they both bid each other goodnight before Clara left the study and disappeared up the stairs.

LooAnne could not wipe the smile from her face as she watched the young maid disappear. When she thought of all that had happened since she had first caught Clara and her secret suitor in the entry hall she found herself amazed. Stephen Parker, the boy she had so diligently warned Clara against, had turned out to be none other than her own twin brother. He had been brought back into her life after she was sure she would never see him again. Not only was he back but he was back for good; the Lord having saved him from the corruption of his cruel family. It was in that moment as she gazed up the stairs that LooAnne took a moment to thank her Heavenly Father for giving her brother back to her, and changing the worst of circumstances into the best.

EIGHTEEN

Days of Our Future

LooAnne stood alone on the back porch of the Nash Estate, looking out over the fields as their tall grasses swayed softly in the early morning breeze. The sun was just beginning to show its face from behind the green mountain, casting a bright tint of pink and red over the sky. Rays of warmth fell through the trees, lighting the dew on the ground so that it glistened. Birds greeted the morning in song; sweet melodies that carried through the air.

LooAnne could see the horses running for the stable doors and the cattle pick up their heads as the ranch hands began to move about on the grounds. She closed her eyes and inhaled deeply, filling her lungs with the crisp morning air and sighing in contentment as a feeling of happiness came over her. Her brother was finally home; after so many days – years even – of worry over the unknown, she finally knew that her twin brother was safe and that he had forgiven her. LooAnne had never harbored such remorse as she did for leaving Stephen alone to face the very people she was running from. Never before or since had she made such a mistake, but now that all was well she determined in her mind never to leave her brother again.

Unable to sleep after the night's happenings LooAnne had finally decided to abandon her bed and watch the sunrise. Even though things seemed so perfect she could still not forget what Peter had said in the stables. She wondered if he regretted it? If he had finally realized the danger in falling for a Luther. LooAnne tried her best to put all thoughts aside as she enjoyed the calming moment of a new day's coming.

Again she closed her eyes, so absorbed in the present sense of calmness that she failed to hear the back door of the estate open behind her, and then a moment later her name was spoken by the same impassive voice that had professed it's love for her only hours before.

"LooAnne."

Startled, LooAnne turned immediately and was very surprised to find herself face to face with the very man who overwhelmed her thoughts; Peter Andrews!

For a moment they stood in silence, both looking at the other, not knowing what to say or indeed what to feel. But Peter could stay silent no longer. "I'm sorry I scared you," he apologized.

LooAnne shook her head, "It's alright," was all her nerves would allow her to say until her eyes landed on Peter's marred face.

"Are-are you alright?" she asked, sincerely wanting to know if the young deputy was well after all that had happened to him.

He nodded, not taking his eyes from her's.

LooAnne began to grow apprehensive under his gaze and spoke again, trying to draw out his words. "I'm sorry you got caught up in all this."

Peter shook his head, "No," he said quietly, as if his mind

wondered elsewhere. "It's not your fault. I..." He didn't finish, his voice trailing off as his eyes dropped to the wooden porch floor beneath them.

"You what?" LooAnne asked after a moment, wanting him to go on.

"I just..." he licked his lips nervously, unsure of what he had intended to tell LooAnne once he was face to face with her. Finally, he decided upon the simplest of words. "What I said was true; I'm in love with you."

LooAnne instantly felt a rush of emotions overcome her as she clapped a hand over her mouth in shock! But Peter did not stop there. "Everything I said in the stables was true," his gaze remained on the ground as he spoke, too afraid of LooAnne's reaction to look her in the eye, "I ain't much for speech makin' as you probably already figured out. I honestly didn't think we were comin' outta that one alive, I thought I wasn't gonna get another chance to tell you how I feel but by the grace of God I did and now I don't know what to say."

A muffled chuckle escaped LooAnne's mouth causing Peter to glance up at her. Seeing the smile she had hidden behind her hand and the light showing brightly in her eyes caused the corner of his mouth to turn up in a grin and gave him the courage to go on.

"I know I'm an idiot," he chuckled, "and there ain't a bone in my body that deserves you. When I first saw you that day you saved me from being beat to death by Cliff, I just had this weird feelin' and it's only gotten bigger since then. I know I'm a fool to think a deputy sheriff has any chance with the niece o' Rick Nash but I been given a second one and I can't waste it."

Peter looked into LooAnne's eyes and she could finally

read the emotion she saw within them. Admiration, love, and hope for his affection returned.

LooAnne found she could discount her own feelings no longer, for they were there, and something told her that Peter Andrews would be worth the risk.

"LooAnne, I know we only met a couple days ago," Peter added when she remained silent, "but we've gotten to know each other a lot over that time and I'm takin' the chance that it was enough to ask you for your permission to come callin'? I ain't in a rush, I know you're worth waiting for, but I want to get to know you better and maybe fall more in love with you if that's even possible," Peter swallowed hard before finishing, "So will you be my girl?"

LooAnne drew in a slow breath, trying to calm the rush of happiness that overcame any hurt she had felt before.

"Yes," she whispered, withdrawing her hand from her mouth. "Of course I will, so long as you forgive me for everything that's happened over the last few days."

Peter smiled but shook his head, "There's nothin' to forgive. I put myself in the situation cause I wanted to help you, it was my decision not your fault. And it was one o' the best decisions I've ever made."

LooAnne's instant smile caused a broad grin to come over Peter's face. He took LooAnne's hand and planted a small kiss on it before saying, "I'll see you at breakfast," and then he was gone.

LooAnne stood still, her eyes locked on the closed door where Peter had been only moments before, her hand tingling as a feeling of warmth overtook her. Part of her good sense told LooAnne to be worried that this would turn out like her previous relationship with Kyle Denson, but all her negative thoughts seemed to be choked out by the overwhelming feeling of happiness and the almost instant surety that Peter was nothing like Kyle.

LooAnne stayed on the porch until the sun had fully risen and then she joined her uncle, Peter, and his parents in the dining room. Clara, however, was not present and it did not take much of LooAnne's imagination to realize where she was. Her father and mother, however, seemed at a loss as to where their daughter had gone to so early in the morning. LooAnne caught Peter's stare and felt herself blush involuntarily before looking down at the table to hide her reddened face.

"Maybe I should go look for her," Mrs. Andrews said in reference to the missing Clara. She was about to rise from her seat when the dining room door was opened and to the foursome's surprise Clara entered with Stephen following behind her!

"Mama, Pa," she said, taking his hand in her's, "Stephen has something he wants to say."

Stephen stepped forward nervously as all eyes landed on him. "Um – Mr. Andrews, I have a confession to make, sir."

Clara's father raised his eye-brows and Stephen continued, "You see, sir, I've been – that is we – um -"

Clara squeezed Stephen's hand and smiled reassuringly at him, urging him to go on. "Um – Clara and I have been – going out – secretly."

Matt Andrews' face instantly took on a look of disapproval, his ire aroused. But before he could speak Clara took to defending Stephen. "It's not entirely his fault, Pa. It was because of his brothers, he was hiding from them and didn't want anyone to know who he was or that he was seeing me. He was trying to protect me."

"Young lady, that ain't no excuse for not telling me and your Ma," Mr. Andrews scolded.

Clara looked down shamefully.

"Sir, we know it was wrong," Stephen spoke up. "At the time I was so afraid that my brothers would find me and maybe hurt Clara that I was too scared to tell anyone."

"But not scared enough to stay away from her to begin with," Mr. Andrews berated.

"I- I know, sir. I'm awful sorry, Mr. Andrews. I swear we didn't mean any harm, that was what we were trying to avoid." Stephen looked down, "And I was afraid you would find out who I was and then I would never have a chance with her. But I do love her, sir, I really do."

"And I love him, Pa," Clara added.

Mr. Andrews shook his head, obviously stunned by this sudden confession and that his daughter had been secretly seeing a member of the Luther family. "How can I condone this? You lied and went behind my back when you should o' come to me first off."

"We know, Pa, and we really are sorry. Please give Stephen a chance? I promise you he's a good man."

"Clara this man you're talking about is the same man who broke into this house last night and fired a shot at Miss Nash and you claim he's a good man?"

"But he is!" Clara insisted. "Last night was a mistake, Pa. Can't a man be allowed one mistake?"

Mr. Andrews shook his head, "Not when that mistake could have well ended the life of another. Now I expect you both to honor my wishes and stay away from each other."

"Excuse me, Pa," Peter spoke up, causing all eyes to turn to him. "I know Stephen made a rotten first impression on you but he's not all bad."

"Peter, he was involved in kidnapping you!" Mrs. Andrews exclaimed.

Peter nodded, "And he kidnapped me to protect Clara. His brothers found out about her and threatened to hurt her if he didn't do what they said. He knew if he went back with them he was just as good as dead but he did anyway. He did it to save Clara's life. Now I ain't sayin' them keepin' that secret was right but he's done a lot for us to be thankful for. I think for that at least he deserves a second chance."

Stephen smiled his thanks to Peter who nodded in return. Mr. Andrews looked at his son thoughtfully and then back at Stephen. After a moment of silent musing he spoke, "I'll give you another chance, young man, but if you so much as look like you're gonna cause Clara, or any of us, any harm I'm gonna have to ask that you stay away from her. And we're gonna be keepin' a very strict eye on you."

Stephen and Clara's faces brightened and they both thanked Mr. Andrews profusely.

Peter then stood from his seat, drawing the attention of everyone in the room. He took a deep breath and said, "Since this seems to be the time I reckon it's my turn," he then turned to Ricky and said, "Mr. Nash, over the last few days I have grown very fond of your niece and I would like to ask your permission to court her. I know you don't know me very well, sir, but I'd like for you and LooAnne to get to know me better. After what happened with Kyle Denson I want you to know that I would never do anything underhanded or for the wrong reasons. I have very strong feelings for LooAnne," he added glancing at LooAnne's blushing face, "and I'd like to hope that she feels the same."

Ricky looked at Peter for a moment, contemplating his next move, and then turned to LooAnne and raised his eyebrows, "Well, my dear?"

LooAnne nodded, "I do, Uncle Ricky. I feel exactly the same way."

Her uncle inhaled deeply and shook his head, "Well, in that case you both have my permission."

LooAnne's face brightened as did Peter's but Ricky was not done yet. He narrowed his eyes at Peter and pointed his finger accusingly, "But you keep in mind that I was the one to throw Kyle through this very window and I won't hesitate to do it again."

Peter's face sobered and he nodded vigorously, "I understand, sir. I promise I won't give you no reason to throw me out the window."

Ricky nodded and Stephen extended his hand to Peter. "You take good care o' my sister, Andrews!"

Peter nodded, "And you take good care of mine, Parker!"

Stephen laughed, and nodded, "I will."

"And so will I."

***

One Year Later:

It was a hot summer morning in early July, the ever growing town of Decatur was packed to capacity for one of the largest events known in its history.

Cliff Luther's trial had long since ended with his conviction of Bill's murder after Karen had finally agreed to identify the man who had threatened her brother. It had taken its toll on the child and her sister but with Dave's ever present comfort and prayers it had not been long before the two let it be known of their engagement and married shortly after. The Nash Estate staff had been true to their promise, none of them having breathed a word of what they knew from the night Stephen had come back; for which LooAnne, Stephen and their uncle were grateful for. Now a prosperous factory director at one of his uncle's businesses, Stephen Parker wasted no time in admitting his wrong to Mr. and Mrs. Andrews and making amends with their daughter; their love for each other only growing as time passed.

Though he had been hesitant at first, Ricky's favor for Peter Andrews grew rapidly and he thanked the Lord for giving his niece the young deputy whose kindness and genuine personality abounded endlessly, as did his love for LooAnne.

The sky was a crisp blue with white clouds floating past the bright sun, a Heavenly inferno beating down on the townspeople and their many guests gathered together in the church yard. Balloons and white streamers decked the church porch, flower pedals sprinkled along the walkway leading to the Nash Sedan which waited on the road.

The church bells rang, the old pipe organ played and the words of the preacher rang out as he united a man and woman in holy matrimony.

"Do you, Stephen Paul Parker, take this woman to be you're lawfully wedded wife, to have and to hold from this day forward; for better or for worse; for richer, for poorer; in sickness and in health; to love and to cherish from this day forward until death do you part?"

Stephen looked down into Clara's dancing blue eyes, his

heart filled with a love for her that he shared with no other. He smiled and nodded, uttering only two words but both of them holding a great meaning. "I do."

Clara's broad smile widened all the more as the preacher continued, "And do you, Clara Olivia Andrews, take this man to be your lawfully wedded husband, to have and to hold from this day forward; for better or for worse; for richer, for poorer; in sickness and in health; to love and to cherish from this day forward until death do you part?" Clara nodded, tears of happiness gathering in her eyes, "I do," she whispered.

Stephen squeezed her hands lovingly as they both turned towards their brother and sister.

"Do you Peter Matthew Andrews take this woman to be your lawfully wedded wife, to have and to hold from this day forward; for better or for worse; for richer, for poorer; in sickness and in health; to love, honor and cherish until death do you part?"

Peter's expression was no longer placid and sullen but full of a new happiness, a new strength of character and purpose beyond his job as deputy sheriff. He was filled with a purpose to love and care for his wife, a feeling he had never experienced before. And LooAnne saw this in his eyes and on his smile as he said, "I do."

"And do you, LooAnne Marie Nash, take this man to be your lawfully wedded husband, to have and to hold from this day forward; for better or for worse; for richer, for poorer; in sickness and in health; to love, honor and obey until death do you part?"

In that moment LooAnne could not help but feel blown away. As she looked into Peter's eyes and recalled all that happened; not only over the past year but since she had first been a child at the Luther Estate, she realized how right her uncle had been when he consoled her after Kyle had left. Peter was one hundred times better than any other man in the world, just as Ricky had said he would be. Never had LooAnne imagined that her intended education would end in finding her lost brother and the love of her life. In times past she had doubted that any man would have her should he know her true identity, but Peter Andrews did and he loved her in spite of it, just as she loved him.

"I do," she nodded, looking into Peter's ocean blue eyes that had not ceased to mesmerize her since the day she had first seen them.

"By the power invested in me I now pronounce you man and wife! Ladies and Gentlemen I present to you Mr. and Mrs. Stephen Parker and Mr. and Mrs. Peter Andrews! Gentlemen, you may kiss your brides!"

A rapturous smile brightened their faces as they sealed the vows with a kiss, savoring the moment and looking forward to the rest of their lives together, forever!

"And what God hath joined together, let no man put asunder."

The End

ONE
Arrival

~

TWO
Belle Hall

~

THREE
Voices in the Night

~

FOUR
First Encounter

~

FIVE
Eavesdropper

~

SIX
Missing...Murder

~

SEVEN
Recognition

~

EIGHT
"I Know"

~

NINE
Taken Together

~

TEN
Stories of a Lifetime

~

ELEVEN
Running!

~

TWELVE
Heart and Soul

~

THIRTEEN
My Brother

~

FOURTEEN
Nightmare

~

FIFTEEN
Emotions Arise

~

SIXTEEN
Love and Lies

~

SEVENTEEN
Making Amends

~

EIGHTEEN
Days of Our Future

~

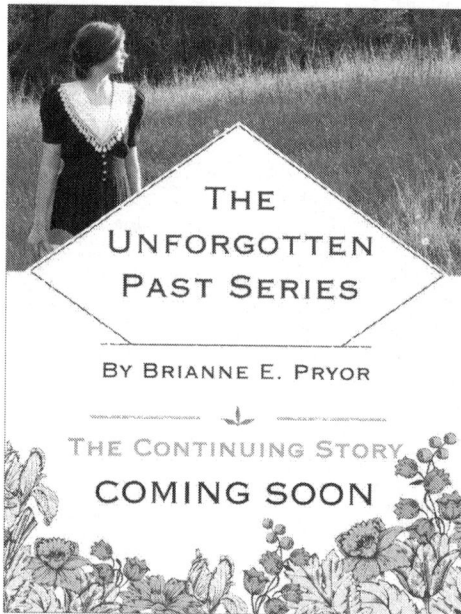

61482062R00137

Made in the USA
Charleston, SC
22 September 2016